The

One hous...

As different in looks as they are in temperament, Alex Conroy and Evan Bellwether became brothers as children when Alex's widowed mother married Evan's father.

Raised to be the Duke of Fallon, Evan's path has looked different from Alex's, who was only recently created the Duke of Glenmoor, but together the two men are ready to take on the *ton*.

Yet when scandal lands Alex's betrothed in Evan's lap (literally), one brother's fate becomes the other's fortune...

Read Evan's story in
Awakening His Shy Duchess

Read Alex's story in
A Duke for the Penniless Widow

Both available now!

Author Note

Since so much of this book is devoted to letters, I might as well tell you about the money-saving, letter-writing practice of the Regency. Since postage increased when more sheets were used, thrifty writers of the nineteenth century wrote the first page of the letter normally. Then, they turned the sheet ninety degrees and wrote the second page over the top of the first.

Cross writing was common in England and the US and was probably even harder to read than my handwriting!

Happy reading,
Christine Merrill

CHRISTINE MERRILL

A Duke for the Penniless Widow

HARLEQUIN®
HISTORICAL™

Recycling programs
for this product may
not exist in your area.

ISBN-13: 978-1-335-59594-2

A Duke for the Penniless Widow

Copyright © 2024 by Christine Merrill

For questions and comments about the quality of this book,
please contact us at CustomerService@Harlequin.com.

Harlequin Enterprises ULC
22 Adelaide St. West, 41st Floor
Toronto, Ontario M5H 4E3, Canada
www.Harlequin.com

Printed in U.S.A.

Christine Merrill lives on a farm in Wisconsin with her husband, two sons and too many pets—all of whom would like her to get off the computer so they can check their email. She has worked by turns in theater costuming and as a librarian. Writing historical romance combines her love of good stories and fancy dress with her ability to stare out the window and make stuff up.

Books by Christine Merrill

Harlequin Historical

"Unwrapped Under the Mistletoe"
in *Regency Christmas Liaisons*
Vows to Save Her Reputation
"Their Mistletoe Reunion"
in *Snowbound Surrender*
The Brooding Duke of Danforth

The Irresistible Dukes

Awakening His Shy Duchess
A Duke for the Penniless Widow

Society's Most Scandalous

How to Survive a Scandal

Secrets of the Duke's Family

Lady Margaret's Mysterious Gentleman
Lady Olivia's Forbidden Protector
Lady Rachel's Dangerous Duke

Visit the Author Profile page
at Harlequin.com for more titles.

To Amanda and Jeremy Olsen
and my new great-nephew, Griffin

Chapter One

Talk of the Ton

After a night of high-stakes play and heavy losses, the unfortunate Mr John Ogilvie returned home and succumbed to despair, ending his life.

Tragedy might have been averted if not for that final hand of cards played with the callous Duke of G., who is known about London for his rapacious appetite for gaming.

Mr Ogilvie leaves a widow and a seven-year-old son.

What will they do now?

And what does G. have to say for himself?

Alex Conroy, the Duke of Glenmoor, stared down at the morning's newspaper in dismay, his finger tracing the item in the gossip column and its veiled references to him. 'I am not callous. I am not rapacious. And I am not at fault. I was there when it happened, of course. But correlation does not imply causation.'

'Your students at Oxford might have been impressed by such a response. But you will have to do better than that to impress the *ton*.' His stepbrother, Evan, shook his head, obviously disappointed at Alex's handling of the situation.

Of course, nothing like this had ever happened to Evan. He had known he would be the Duke of Fallon from the moment he'd known anything. He had received a lifetime's training in navigating London society and had no trouble keeping his name from the scandal sheets, other than the brief hubbub created by his sudden marriage.

But Alex had never expected to inherit a title. The death of an heirless cousin had resulted in his sudden elevation to a dukedom, a move that had left him scrambling to keep up with the new expectations put upon him and the prurient interest of strangers in the intimate details of his life.

Alex tapped the paper again. 'This makes it sound as if I drove a man to his death. That was not what happened at all.'

Evan sighed. 'As you should know from my marriage, it is not what *happened* that matters. What people *think* happened is far more important. Since you are relatively new to your title and were not expected to be heir to it, everyone wonders what sort of a peer you will make. They will watch you and they will read the gossip.'

'But this makes me out to be some kind of monster,' Alex said with a weak laugh. 'You know I am hardly the sort to push a man into risky wagers just to see him suffer.'

'I know it. But others may not,' Evan replied with another shake of his head. 'Unless they were there, all people will know is that, after losing a card game with "the Duke of G.", Mr John Ogilvie went home and blew his brains out.'

Alex winced. It was an accurate way to describe what had happened. But he could not help but wish that Evan had chosen a more polite euphemism to screen the truth. 'I did not know that the man had a problem with gambling. I thought it was a friendly round of loo to pass the time.'

And it had been just that. There had been nothing to distinguish this particular game from hundreds of other hands he had played in his life. The stakes were not particularly high and the other men at the table good-humoured. Even Ogilvie had seemed in high spirits and not the desperate man that he must have been.

'Earlier in the evening he had been banned from another gaming hell for his erratic play,' Evan said, repeating a truth that was common knowledge now that the gossip rags had got hold of the story.

'I did not know he'd already lost his savings and his house,' Alex said. 'Why did he not stop at that? Why did he insist on playing with me?'

Evan shrugged. 'Perhaps he thought his luck would turn.'

'And it was not even that great a loss. Fifty pounds…'

'That is more than some of my tenants make in a year,' Evan said gently.

'It was more than I'd planned to bet,' Alex agreed. 'But the fellow kept raising the stakes.'

'Trying to win back enough to stall the inevitable. By the time he got to you, there was nothing left to cover his loss. Fifty was the same as a thousand fifties to him.'

'Had he but asked, I'd have torn up his marker and thought nothing more about it. It was only a game…'

'Pride prevented him,' Evan said with a sigh. 'And the same pride caused him to take his own life rather than admit to his wife and son what he had done.'

This was even worse. The knowledge that a family was suffering as a result of what he had done was almost more than Alex could bear.

'Since you were the only titled man at that last card game, you are the one to take the blame,' Evan said, heaping guilt upon guilt.

'It is not fair,' Alex blurted, feeling like a selfish fool as he imagined the widow and child and what they must be feeling.

'I said something rather like that when I was forced to marry last Season,' Evan said with a smile. 'And you reminded me that it was not about what was fair, it was about what was proper.'

'That was an entirely different matter,' Alex said quickly. 'People thought your scandal was romantic. But this?' He picked the paper up and threw it into the fire. 'They will think me a murderer.'

'Some will,' Evan agreed. 'But the rumours fade with time. I would avoid the gaming tables for a while to prove that you are not going to make a habit of leading men to their ruin.'

Alex nodded in agreement. 'And I must see if there is anything to be done for the widow Ogilvie. It is not right that she and her son are to be turned out into the street because of her husband's folly.'

'A measure of forgiveness from her would go a long way towards mending your reputation,' Evan said.

It would salve his conscience as well. Though Alex knew he was largely innocent of what had happened with Ogilvie, he could not say he was totally blameless. If he had cried off the game, perhaps the fellow would still be alive. But he'd had no reason to. Perhaps Mrs Ogilvie would find it in her heart to reassure him. 'I will go to her. At the very least, I can give her the damned marker back and release her from a small portion of his debt.'

Then he could come home and begin the process of forgetting that this tragedy had ever happened.

It was Selina Ogilvie's first real day as a widow.

Though her husband had died three days ago, those first days had hardly counted. A hush had fallen over the house in the minutes after the discovery of the body. But when it had ended, there had been a flurry of activity that had not stopped since.

First, the housekeeper had sent for a physician, which had been thoughtful but pointless. It was quite clear to anyone that looked that her husband was far beyond the need of one. All Dr Crawford did to help was to try to force laudanum on Selina, which was even more pointless. She was stunned, but in no way hysterical.

If anything, she was angry. The least John could have done before ending his life was to have written her a note of apology. Instead, he had used his final moments to make a record of his losses, a carefully annotated list of markers and IOUs that contained the deed to the house and all the money in the bank. Then, as if he could not decide what to do about the debts, he had put a pistol to his head and exited life's stage, leaving the problem to her.

If she was asleep as Crawford wished her to be, who would take control of the household? There was no family on either side that would help. She had been an orphan when they'd married. And by his erratic behaviour and requests for loans, her husband had destroyed any family bonds or friendships that might have yielded aid in this difficult time. Judging by his final ledger, there was not a person she could think of that he had not already borrowed money from.

So she had done the only thing she could think of and sent her maid to pawn her jewels to pay for the funeral and to keep the house in groceries for as long as she could. Then she had gone upstairs to explain to little Edward that he would never see his father again.

With the arrangements to be made and the visit to the church, there had been no time to think about herself and her new status as a woman alone in the world. But now the study was cleaned, the body was buried and quiet had descended again. All the emotions she had kept at bay for those few days had come flooding back, threatening to engulf her.

The worst part of it was the change in the quality of the visitors. At the start, there had been a thin trickle of bereavement calls from acquaintances making vague offers of help and looking thoroughly relieved when she did not ask for any. But today's callers were the men who held the bulk of her husband's debt. She had been asked how she meant to pay, when and how much and, worst of all, when she was planning to vacate this house, which she no longer had the right to inhabit.

Mr Baxter, the house's new owner, stood before her now, staring at her with an unctuous smile and patting the pocket that held the deed. 'It is an unfortunate matter, Mrs Ogilvie. Most unfortunate. But it is a debt of honour and I am sure your husband would want to see it paid.'

She was tempted to shout that if John had wanted to see it, he would still be here. But it was clear that a display of temper would do nothing to move this man. Perhaps she could appeal to his sympathy. 'I am aware of that, sir. And I do mean to make good on all my husband's losses. But the current moment is a difficult one. John has only just died and there were arrangements to be made and the funeral to think of. We have not yet had time to look for new lodgings.' She added a hopeful smile to hint that it was in his power to give them time, if he chose.

He returned a smile so reptilian she expected to see a forked tongue dart into the middle of it. 'I am aware that it has been a difficult week. But I am sure, if you are amenable, an arrangement might be made that would allow you to stay here as long as you like.' He blinked once, then stared at her, his expression unchanging, and added, 'As long as we are both satisfied, at least.' Then he waited.

She stared back at him, shocked. He could not be suggesting what she suspected. But there was something in the sibilant hiss of the word *satisfaction* that made his meaning clear.

'If you are worrying about your son,' he added, 'you needn't. There are many schools that take in indigent students as a charity. He would be away most of the year and would not need to know.'

'That was not what I was worried about,' she said, 'because I have no intention of taking your despicable offer. I cannot believe that you would come here, when my husband's body is barely cold, and suggest that I…I…' She could not finish the sentence with anything more than a shudder.

'I am only suggesting what others will suggest, when you tell them that you do not have the money they are owed,' he said in a reasonable tone. 'You are only angry with me because I am the first. But once you realise the depth of your troubles and once you have weighed the solutions available, you might feel quite differently.'

'I will not,' she said.

He shrugged. 'Then you must tell me when you plan to be out of the house. I could perhaps wait until the end of the week, if you can be packed in that time.'

'It will take at least until the end of the month to auction off the furnishings,' she said with a frozen smile. 'Unless you mean to take those as well.'

When he seemed to be considering the idea, she added, 'Since they are not listed as part of what you are owed, I will have them appraised and you can pay me by cheque.'

'That will not be necessary,' he said, his eyes narrowing at the prospect of parting with money over something that was not her. 'You may have until the end of the month, Mrs Ogilvie. And in that time, if you have reconsidered my offer, you may reach me here.' He reached into his pocket and withdrew a calling card, which he set on a side table. 'For now, good day.'

'Goodbye, Mr Baxter,' she said emphatically, sinking into the nearest chair as he left her alone in the sitting room. As much as it disgusted her to admit the truth, he was probably right. He would not be the last to suggest that she work off her husband's debt while on her back. She was still young, and handsome enough to attract unwanted attention. Some people would assume that, simply because she was a widow, she would be eager to have a man in her life, with or without the sanctity of marriage.

As if she would seek more trouble, after the mess her husband had left her in. The idea made her want to laugh, but she was afraid if she did, she might never stop. It was either that or cry from sheer frustration. Was she to be allowed no time to grieve at all?

But if she did not mean to bend to an unsavoury

offer, how was she to manage to pay off the rest of the creditors? This afternoon, she would have to contact an auction house, just as she had said, and begin the process of liquidating her life in the hopes that there was enough to balance the books. Then she would have to let the servants go and search for a place where she and Edward could start over, though she had no idea where they would get the money to do so. What was she to do?

The thought brought on the first tears she had shed since John had died, and she allowed herself the luxury of letting them fall.

'Mrs Ogilvie?' Her housekeeper appeared in the doorway.

'What is it?' she said, quickly wiping the tears away.

'You have another visitor.' The woman gave her a worried look. 'The Duke of Glenmoor.'

The man who had all but killed her husband had decided to collect his debt in person, just as Baxter had. Selina sucked in her breath, her tears forgotten in a flash of anger. 'Tell him I am not at home to him.'

The words were barely out of her mouth before she saw the man just behind the servant, waiting to be announced. He was standing between her and escape, in plain sight and hearing of her attempted snub. Now he was staring at her just as Baxter had done and probably thinking the same thing: that she was alone and vulnerable to improper suggestions.

She glared back at him, her despair turning to anger. She had no experience with the peerage. When she had ventured out into society, her acquaintances had been far more modest, limited to untitled ladies and gentlemen and a few moderately successful cits. But the man who stood before her now was everything she would have imagined a duke would be.

His tailoring was perfect, his linen immaculate. Together they framed a body that was impressively tall and in peak physical condition. His short hair shone dark and shiny against a face that was unmarked by sun or worry. His eyes were dark as well, a rich sherry brown, and their alert gaze was fixed on her as if she was a problem in want of a solution.

In any other circumstance, she'd have been impressed by his rank and cowed by his good looks, stunned into submission by the sheer elegance of him and too aware of how far beneath his notice she must seem. She would also have been more than a little flattered by the intensity of his interest in her.

But not today. She had no intention of bowing down to the man who had ruined her life, or blushing and simpering like some idiot girl at her first ball. 'What do you want?' She spat the words at him, taking the offensive to prove that she was not about to be taken advantage of in her lowest moment.

'I… I came to help,' he said, taking a half-step back as if to move out of range of her ire.

'You have done quite enough already,' she said with a bitter smile, reminding herself that, though his appearance was pleasant, he was also the man who had fleeced her husband. 'I have you to thank for my current position. What more could you possibly do?'

'I…' Was it her imagination, or had her accusation

hurt him? There was something in his dark eyes and
the set of his too-perfect mouth that hinted at injury.

If so, he deserved it. Compared to her own pain,
his was nothing. 'You,' she said, sneering back at him,
'have done quite enough, thank you. But I suppose
you will be wanting me to settle my husband's debt to
you. It is a matter of honour and I know how important that is to a man of your stature.' She let the last
drip with irony, to remind him of what he had done.

Then she reached to her throat, her fingers grasp-
ing the jet cameo brooch she wore as a symbol of
her mourning. 'Here.' She pulled it free. 'If this is
not worth fifty pounds, it will have to do. It is all I
have left.' Then she threw it at him with all the force
she could muster.

He snatched it out of the air with a graceful swipe
of his hand and said, 'I am sorry.'

'You should be,' she snapped back, feeling the unshed tears prickling the backs of her eyes, ready to fall
at the least provocation. She would not show weakness. She did not dare to, or she would be preyed upon
by every unscrupulous man in London.

And this one was the worst of the lot, because his
offer would not be as obviously repellent as Baxter's
had been. He had been a serpent, but this man was
Lucifer incarnate, proud and beautiful and all too
tempting.

Staring too closely into those lovely eyes or focusing too long on that perfect mouth would weaken her
reserve. The proposition that he was likely to make
would be surrounded by sweet words and delivered

with a gentle smile and a soothing voice. If she was not careful, she would agree to the unspeakable and think herself lucky. She should get far away from him as fast as possible, before she forgot that she had nothing left but her honour and bartered it away.

She must not run, or he would know how he affected her and use that knowledge against her. Instead, she rose slowly and walked to the door with her head held high, pushed past him and mounted the main stairs, never looking back until she reached the safety of her bedroom and had locked the door behind her.

Chapter Two

Mrs Ogilvie was a startlingly attractive woman. Far too pretty to be alone for long.

It was a horrible thing to think at such a time. Her husband was barely gone. She was distraught and thought he was the cause of it. He was ashamed of himself for letting his mind wander in such a direction.

But as Alex had looked at her, he'd felt he was falling into her huge grey eyes, caught in them like the tears that trembled on their lashes. He wanted to gather her to him, to stroke her smooth blonde hair and assure her that he would take care of everything, if she would only let him.

He'd even buy her proper mourning attire, if that was what she wanted. Her lavender gown had been a cheerful day dress until someone had hurriedly tacked black ribbons to the ruffles to signify her bereavement and added the black brooch she had thrown at him as a final touch. But no amount of crêpe could dim her loveliness, her vivacity and her obviously passionate nature.

He shook his head, surprised at the insensitive thoughts in it. He knew it was the worst time for him to notice such things. A new widow did not want to hear that she would have no trouble replacing the man she was grieving for. She certainly did not want to hear anything of the sort from a man who held her husband's debts.

It was probably just as well that he had been stunned near to silence at the sight of her loveliness. He was normally very good with words, perfectly capable of speaking up for himself in any given situation. But today, as he'd stared at her, he'd been unable to string two thoughts together.

Judging by her response to what little he'd said, she had not wanted to hear anything at all and had assumed the worst about his character and his offer to help. Alex stared down at the cameo he held and wondered what sort of visits she had already been paid. Had men been making improper suggestions to her?

If they had not, they soon would be. She was far too pretty to end up in a workhouse or as a charitable ward of some church or other. Men often made discreet arrangements with widows, offering to fulfil both their physical and financial needs in one go. Judging by the reports in the paper and her current distress, her monetary problems would soon outweigh any qualms she might have about accepting such an offer.

His hand tightened on the brooch until the pin pricked his finger. It was unfair. A woman like that should be offered marriage.

Not by him, of course. He had the succession to think of and she had a son already. The last thing he wanted was to bring up some small boy the way he'd been brought up himself, as the unwanted spare in a house with a legitimate heir.

His own widowed mother had not thought twice about accepting an offer from the Duke of Fallon, leaving him in the curious position of having a stepbrother who was both younger and already a marquis. Though he had got on well enough with Evan, his stepfather had made it clear from the first moment of the marriage that Alex was worthless and unwelcome, not really a part of the family at all.

The old Duke had been long dead when Alex had inherited a title of his own. But he doubted, even if old Fallon had known his future, it would have changed the way he'd treated the superfluous son he had acquired along with his marriage.

But none of this mattered. Mrs Ogilvie would not have him, even if he asked. She loathed him for the part he had played in her husband's downfall and blamed him, just as society did. She had rushed from the room to avoid him, leaving him stunned and silent with her housekeeper, who was trying to raise the nerve to put him out of the house.

He looked down at the cameo in his hand, then fished his other hand into his pocket for the marker Ogilvie had given him just before he'd ended his life. He tore the thing in half and folded the pieces around the brooch, handing it to the servant with a sympathetic smile. 'When she is feeling better, give this to

Mrs Ogilvie with my assurance that she is free from this debt, at least.'

Then he let himself out.

His carriage was waiting, the servants jumping to attention at the sight of him, a fact he was not used to, though he'd come into his title almost a year ago. 'I wish to walk,' he said to the coachman.

'Very well, Your Grace,' the man said with a worried look.

Then he set out towards home, the carriage following just behind him. The wheeled escort spoiled the solitude he'd wished for, but that was the problem with a large staff. One could never be totally alone.

The distance to his home was over two miles, but that was nothing. Or at least it had been when he'd been a humble don at Oxford and his feet had been his only mode of transport. London life was making him soft. Slow-witted as well.

In the past, he was sure he'd have been able to come up with the words to placate the woman he'd just met. There had to be something he could do to make her life easier. He was, in part, responsible for the situation she found herself in. Not to the degree that society accused him of being and certainly not in the way she thought. But he was not blameless.

There had to be something he could do.

As he walked down the street, the words echoed in his head and, slowly, a plan formed. By the time he'd reached his home, he had decided on a course of action. He handed his hat and gloves to the doorman with a nod of thanks and went directly to his study, sitting down at the desk and searching the drawers for the right sort of paper. He needed something plain, not the fine stationery that he used for Glenmoor's correspondence. The crest on that would give the game away before it was begun.

With an unembossed white sheet before him, he began to write.

Dear Mrs Ogilvie,
I am sorry to hear of the misfortune that has befallen you and offer sincere condolences on the death of your husband and the situation it has left you in.
I consider myself a friend of your family and hope that the enclosed will be of some help. If, as I suspect, you are in greater need and wish further aid, write to me care of the General Post Office and I will be honoured to assist you.
Sincerely,

He paused. He could not very well put his own name on the letter or she would throw it away unopened. Worse yet, she would open it and form an opinion of him that was even worse than she already had. She would be convinced, as she had suggested earlier, that he wanted something more than absolution.

But if not himself, then who should he be?

He turned and glanced at the shelves behind his chair and the books arranged alphabetically upon them by author. The first had ABBOTT neatly lettered in gold on the lower spine. Did he know anyone by that name? Was there anyone involved in the Ogilvie matter who would answer to it?

He could not think of any. And he could think of no more innocent nom de plume, for this one had a monastic sound to it that might assure her of his innocent intentions. So, he signed with a flourish at the bottom of the letter.

Mr Abbott

He blotted the ink and unlocked the top drawer where he kept a money box, opening it and counting out a stack of ten-pound notes on to the paper. Then he folded them in and sealed the letter with a plain blob of red wax before setting it with the rest of the outbound mail.

He smiled down at it, satisfied. Perhaps this was not the best solution, but it would allow him to sleep at night if he knew the fascinating woman he had met today would be free, at least for a time, to make her first decisions as a widow without the immediate and overwhelming pressure of poverty.

Then he went back to his desk to take care of the usual day's business.

Selina waited in her room a full hour after her meeting with the Duke, not coming down again until she was sure she was composed. To maintain calm below stairs, there must be no sign of chaos above stairs. Since her husband's death, she had already lost two housemaids, one of whom had taken a pair of silver teaspoons by way of severance. Crying and panic on her part might lead to a mass exodus tomorrow. Since she was not sure of her future, she wanted to maintain a stable present for as long as she could.

She returned to her place in the sitting room, praying that there might be some small light in a future that seemed uniformly black.

When the afternoon post arrived, she looked at the stack of letters with dread. The morning's had contained more bills than she'd known they received, many of them past due. This was likely to be more of the same. But at the bottom was a surprisingly thick packet addressed to her in an unfamiliar hand.

She took the lot to the morning room and opened the strange letter first, surprised to see a pile of bank notes flutter to the floor as she broke the seal. She scooped them up again, counting the money and stacking it neatly upon the writing table. Fifty pounds. Enough to pay the household bills for weeks. Her problems were bigger than that, of course. But at least the servants would stop leaving and give her time to think.

She read the note, then read it again, searching for any clue as to the identity of the mysterious Mr Abbott. Her husband had never mentioned the name, nor could she think of any Abbotts in her own limited acquaintance. There was no close family living on either side and she racked her brain for distant cousins named Abbott, but there were none.

If this man was not family or friend, there was no telling who he was, or what his motives might be if they were not as compassionate as they appeared.

If she did not want to be in debt to a stranger, she could not keep the money. She should not. And yet…

She pulled a sheet of paper out of the drawer and began a letter of her own.

Dear Sir,

She stared down at the blank paper for a moment and then wrote what she thought.

I was stunned to receive your letter and your most generous gift. However, no matter how kind the intention, it is very improper and I cannot encourage it. Ladies, if they wish to think of themselves as such, do not take money from strangers because of the assumed reckoning that comes with such gifts and the fear of finding oneself beholden to a man with less than honourable intentions.

She stared down at the sentence for a moment, wondering what he would think if his motives were truly as innocent as he claimed. Then she added:

Not that I am accusing you of such. It is just that, should the rumour get around that I am taking money from gentlemen, it will attract the sort of men who see it as a weakness and wish

*to put me in the difficult position of refusing
their advances.*

She nodded in approval at this, for it sounded very
proper, then stared at the stack of banknotes he had
sent her. This was the point where she should close
the letter and fold the money into it, before sending
the lot back to him, whoever he was. But if she kept
it, it would buy her enough time to find a new home
and a new life. She set the money aside and started
her concluding paragraph.

*And that is why I can accept no further gifts
from you. Thank you so much for your consideration, but I am sure, with time, things will
get better for me.*

It was a lie, of course. She had no idea how she
would manage. But there was no reason to tell that to
a man who she did not even know. She closed.

*Sincerely,
Mrs John Ogilvie*

If he was a stranger, he was not entitled to her
Christian name. And though he was no longer living, the presence of John in the letter would tell him
she was not already angling for a relationship outside of marriage.

Satisfied, she carried the letter to the hall table to
go out with the next post.

* * *

Alex tried not to show his excitement as the servant he had sent to enquire at the post office handed him the letter, stacking it carefully with the rest of his mail and taking it to the study to read. She had written back. And she had done it quickly, for her answer came to him the morning after he had written to her.

He had known that there was a possibility that he would hear nothing from her, not even a brief thank you. He did not think there was anything specific in the rules of etiquette about replying to anonymous benefactors, but he suspected it was rather like encouraging the attentions of strange men and was frowned upon.

But it appeared that Mrs Ogilvie was both brave and curious. He liked that about her, just as he liked her fine grey eyes and trim figure.

As soon as the door was closed and he was alone, he moved her letter back to the top of the stack and tore at the seal to reveal the brief message within.

She did not think she could take the money?

He allowed himself a short silent laugh. He noticed she had not sent it back. It meant that, even against her better judgement, his instincts were right. She needed his help. She would accept further aid with a little more pressure and he could keep her safe from the inappropriate offers she feared, until she was ready to marry again.

But would it be wise to write her again?

Her letter had laid out the dangers of it and he could not contradict a word of it. If someone discovered that he was keeping her, they would assume the worst about her and about him.

As for his own reputation, he did not care. After the incident with Ogilvie it was clear that the papers would assume the worst about him no matter what he did.

And for her, surely it would be better to be thought a whore than having to become one in truth. If he was very careful and they had no other contact that might arouse suspicions, there would be no danger of either. He would simply watch over her for a time, make sure she was provided for, then fade from her life once she had found a new husband to care for her properly.

He sharpened a pen and pulled a blank sheet of paper out of the desk drawer to scribble out an answer.

My dear Mrs Ogilvie,
I completely understand your hesitance to ac-
cept my gift and reiterate my assurance that I
require nothing from you in return.

As far as society's suspicions when a gentle-
man attempts to help a lady that is not of his
family? In my opinion, they can and should
be damned for their wicked interpretation of
simple generosity. There are people who insist
on believing the worst in others. Pray do not
sink to their level.

If you are called by such people to explain
the sudden change in your fortunes, tell them
that an aged uncle has left you an inheritance
and say nothing more about the matter.

*To make the disbursement of funds easier, I
am setting up an account in your name at Bar-
clay's. Feel free to draw on it as needed and
write to me with further requests.
Sincerely,*

He paused for a moment, then added,

Old Uncle Abbott

He smiled, nodding in approval. He rather liked
being avuncular. There was something uniquely
harmless about it. Friendly as well, though he could
not remember anything particularly kind or help-
ful about his own uncles when they had been alive.
Perhaps it was only imaginary uncles who exhibited
those qualities.

He put his quill back in the stand and folded the
letter, reaching automatically for the signet ring in
his drawer before remembering to leave the wax seal
blank. Then he dropped the finished letter in the outgoing post.

Chapter Three

'It has been a year since John died. That is more than enough time to grieve a man who treated you well and far too long to honour John Ogilvie. It is time you looked for another husband. You are not getting any younger.' Selina's friend Mary Wilson was giving her a candid look as if searching for signs of decrepitude. They were taking their daily walk in Hyde Park and the bright sunlight of the morning was sure to highlight imperfections in the complexion that were usually hidden.

'John did not treat me badly. At least, he did not intend to. And I am twenty-seven,' Selina replied with a laugh, tipping her face to the sky in defiance. 'Some men think that I am already too old for marriage.'

'Who has told you that you are getting old?' Mary said, outraged on her behalf.

'Other than you, just now?' Selina reminded her. 'No one in particular. But you must admit that the majority of women my age are already settled, one way or another, and have already given up on husband-hunting. If you look to the members of the Ladies' Mathematical Society, you will notice a pattern. The single women my age in those meetings are all confirmed spinsters.'

'But you are prettier than they are,' Mary said with a grin. 'And how did you find yourself in that crowd in the first place? You will forgive me for saying so, but your interests do not seem to lie with mathematics.'

'I received an invitation from an acquaintance,' she said, hoping that Mary would not question the identity of that person. 'Someone who suggested that it was time for me to break my solitude and re-enter society.'

'Well, I am glad that you listened, or we would never have met,' Mary said. 'Now, we must find other invitations that will bring you a step further out and into the company of eligible men.'

Though Abbott had been eager to see her seek friendships with women of her set, he had done nothing yet to relaunch her into mixed society. Perhaps he expected her to fend for herself when it came to finding a husband. Or perhaps it was because he was jealous and wished to keep her for himself. She hoped that was it for she certainly did not want to spoil the unique intimacy of their correspondence by seeking another man.

In the year since he had first written, they had grown quite close. And though he insisted that he was unwilling or unable to meet her, she could not help but imagine there might someday be something more between them than letters. The thought made her smile, as she so often did when she thought of him.

Now Mary was giving her an appraising look, as if she had revealed something without speaking. 'Do not tell me that there is someone already.'

Selina forced a laugh. 'No one but my dear little Edward.'

'Are you sure? Because for a moment, there was a look in your eyes that was quite…' Mary gave a wave of her hand to express the inexpressible.

'No one, I assure you,' she lied. No one she could point to, anyway.

Mary looked around them, changing the subject. 'And where is your dear little Edward, by the way? I do not see him on the path ahead.'

Nor was he behind, when Selina turned to look. At times like this she wished ladies were allowed to curse, for sometimes it seemed that was what her son wanted her to do. 'He is probably just out of sight,' she said with more confidence than she felt. 'Edward!' She raised her voice so that it might be heard from a distance, but kept the tone light to avoid frightening him into hiding.

When there was no answer, she turned around, scanning in all directions, hoping that there would be some sign of him that she had missed before. Then she increased her pace, hurrying up the path to search for him.

As they walked, she shot Mary a look of false confidence. 'I am sure we will see him around the next turn. He cannot have got far.' But the last time that he had wandered off, it had taken over an hour to find him. That time, he had been lost as well as disobedient, and when he'd managed to return to her, they were both quite frightened.

But today it seemed that there would be no such trouble. As they rounded a bend Edward was stumbling back down the path towards her, his eyes focused on something he held in his hand rather than where he was placing his feet.

'Where have you been?' she said, hurrying to his side.

'I followed a squirrel and when I looked up, you were gone.' Then he glanced up at her, smiling, oblivious to her panic. 'But this works.' He held out his hand to her, showing her the item he held.

It was a brass compass, about two inches in diameter. 'Where did you get this?'

'A man gave it to me,' he said with a grin. 'He asked me if I was lost and told me if I pointed the arrow to North and walked towards the SW, I would find you again. And I did.' His grin broadened.

'We must find him and return this,' she said, holding out her hand for the thing.

'He said I was to keep it, as it was so near my birthday,' he said, closing his fingers around it to prevent her from taking it away. 'And that when I wander off, like I did last week, I must use this to keep track of where I was going.'

Abbott.

He was the only man she could think of who would know Edward's birthday and had been told about his habit of wandering off. And, as with so many of her problems, he had found a solution before she could think to ask for it.

Her breath caught in her throat as she realised the most important thing about this interaction. He was here. Or, at least, he had been. She looked around at the other men on the path, wondering if he was still nearby. 'Where is he?' she said, gripping Edward by the shoulder, then forcing herself to relax so as not to alarm him. 'I wish to thank him for helping you.'

'He walked away,' her son said, more interested in the compass than he was in the conversation.

He had been so close, but he had gone before she could see him. 'This man,' she said, struggling to stay calm, 'what did he look like?'

'He was old,' Edward replied, without looking up.

She nodded, trying not to look disappointed by the fact. He had the wisdom of a man in later life. There was no reason to think of him as anything but the uncle he had first pretended to be.

'Old like you,' her son added, and her spirits immediately lifted.

'What colour was his hair? Was it grey?'

'Brown.'

She smiled. He was not too old, then. 'And his eyes. What colour were they? Was he wearing spectacles? Was he tall? Did he walk with a cane?'

At this rush of questions, Edward gave her a confused look, then said, 'He was just a man. In a dark coat,' he added, as if this would help. Then he held the compass out to her again. 'Can I keep it? Is it all right?'

She sighed, for it was clear that she would get no more information than she had already. Then she held out her hand. 'Let me see it for a moment.'

He handed it to her and she turned it over, surprised to see the initials *M* and *C* engraved on the back.

'He said it was his father's,' Edward said, shifting from foot to foot, clearly eager to have it back.

'That means the initials are not his,' she said. Of course, the second would be. He would share his father's surname. But there was no reason to suspect that either of his names was Abbott. He had admitted long ago that it was a pseudonym.

None of this should matter. When they had begun their correspondence, he had made it clear from the first that they would never be more than friends.

But after a year of writing, she had grown to hope.

Next to her, Mary laughed. 'So, there is someone, after all. Do not deny it, for I can tell by the light in your eyes that there is.'

'Perhaps,' she admitted, staring down the path at no one in particular. 'At least, there could be. But he has made no promises, as of yet.'

'Is he married?' Mary whispered.

'I do not know,' she whispered back. 'We have only written.'

But there had been so many letters. Never more than a week had separated them for the whole of the year and sometimes they had written two or more in a single day. 'And yet, we have never met,' she added, unable to stop the sigh that escaped from her parted lips.

'How romantic,' Mary said with a sigh of her own.

'Not really,' she said, trying to regain control of the conversation again. 'We are friends, that is all. We have never really discussed our feelings beyond that. And no promises have been made,' she added, lest Mary think he was dishonourable. 'Nor has he made any demands on me, if that is what you fear.'

Mary laughed again. 'I fear no such thing.' She glanced down at Edward, who was too busy with his new possession to pay any mind to their conversation. 'In fact, a few demands might be just the thing you need.'

'I beg your pardon?' Selina said, with a blush that proved she knew exactly what her friend was suggesting.

Mary gave her a knowing look. 'I am only saying that, should my husband die, there are some things that I would quite miss in his absence, especially if it had been a whole year.'

It had been some time longer than that, if Selina wished to be honest, which she did not. In the last months of his life, her John had been far more interested in cards and dice than he had been in any comfort she might offer. And Mary was right; she was lonely. 'But what you are talking about has nothing to do with the gentleman we are discussing. Our friendship is purely intellectual.'

'And these cerebral conversations are what puts that colour in your cheeks,' Mary said with obvious scepticism.

'Yes,' she said, in what she hoped was a convincing tone. Then added, 'It is simply rather exciting to know that he was so close.'

'Yet he did not bother to meet with you,' Mary concluded for her, as if trying to dash her hopes. 'Judging by Edward's description, he is not old, or infirm, or scarred in a way that would frighten a small child.'

'Hmm…' Selina replied, trying to pretend that she had not considered just those possibilities. Her favourite theory, that of a disfiguring war injury, had been discounted by today's meeting. Though she had often imagined that she would love him just as much if he were missing an eye or some other important part of his body.

'Even though there is nothing obviously wrong with him, he has made no effort to advance your friendship into a courtship,' Mary said, considering. 'I suspect that means he is a married man and should not be writing to you at all.'

That was her greatest fear. That the reason he had been so reticent in declaring himself was that he was permanently beyond her reach. 'Our letters are perfectly innocent,' she insisted. At least, the ones she had posted were. There had been others, ones that she had written but not sent, where she had expressed her true feelings. These she kept neatly folded in her empty jewellery case, a tidy packet of billets-doux to take the place of the ones she had never received.

Mary sighed again, ignoring her protestations. 'It is still quite exciting. Too exciting to be proper, of course. You must find out who the man is. Then you will know if you should continue writing to him.'

It was good that she had not mentioned the money she had been given, for she was sure Mary would not have approved of that. 'I will ask him to reveal himself in the very next letter,' she lied, then changed the subject.

Alex sorted through the afternoon post, tucking the expected letter from Selina into the pocket of his coat and walking slowly towards the study, where he could enjoy it in private. He was eager to see her response to the gift he had given her son, hoping she did not think him too forward.

It was one thing to provide her with enough money to run her household, but quite another for him to approach Edward in person without bothering to ask her permission. Of course, he had not asked her leave before he'd begun to provide for her and had ignored her initial refusals, allowing the desperation of her situation to wear down any arguments about propriety.

And, as he too often did when thinking about the details of their arrangement, he felt a growing sense of unease. No one had uncovered their relationship, as of yet. But it had been a year and his luck would not last forever. He should reveal himself to her before someone else did it for him and hope that she could find her way to forgive him for the part he'd played in her husband's downfall.

Most importantly, he must find a way to end their relationship without damaging her reputation. What he had done had not been at her suggestion and he would not have strangers thinking her mercenary or unchaste for accepting his help. The last thing he wanted was to leave her in a worse place than he had found her.

He would have to leave her. That was inevitable. She deserved a man in her life and in her bed and, given their past, he would never be able to give her more than money and this unusual friendship. But he could tell from the carefully veiled hints in her letters that she had developed a tendre for him and was hoping that there could be something more than there was between them.

He understood the feeling. When he'd met her, he'd thought her the most beautiful of women. But their correspondence had revealed a spirit that suited her looks. She was inquisitive, intelligent and made him laugh.

As he read her letters, he heard the resonant alto of her voice, soft as velvet against skin, murmuring the words to him. At night, when the letters were put away, he imagined them together in body as well as spirit, making love to exhaustion, then whispering their hopes and dreams to each other as the sun rose on a new day.

When morning came again, he would remember what 'the Duke of G.' had done to her and her family and how she had looked at him, the one time he'd tried to help in person. If they had been any two other people, he would have revealed himself by now and made an offer. But she was who she was and he was the very thing she hated in all the world.

He smiled sadly down at the letter in his hand. At least, for a little while, he could be someone else. He ran a finger along the edge of the paper in his pocket, sighing as he drew it out. Then he popped the seal and began to read.

My dear Abbott,

He smiled again, pressing a thumb over the words and imagining her writing them, smiling back at him.

I am just back from Hyde Park and I must know the truth. You were there, weren't you? You spoke to Edward and sent him back to me when he strayed. The gift you gave him was most kind and very practical. I have been regaled with the compass points of each room in our little house and he is now out in the garden, mapping the flowers as they orient to true north.

He could imagine that as well, for he had done something similar when his father had given him the same tool, at about the same age.

But the gift would have been even better if you had followed him back to me and come home with us for tea.

'Or so you think,' he said with a sad shake of his head, and read on.

My friend Mrs Wilson was with us and noted my excitement and I could not avoid telling her about our correspondence. She expressed concern that you are already married and avoiding me so as not to give offence. Please tell me honestly, is there a Mrs Abbott? Perhaps you could bring that fortunate lady with you when you visit, so I might know her as well.

He reached for the paper that sat ready on the corner of his desk and sharpened his pen to craft a response.

My dear Mrs Ogilvie,

He whispered 'Selina' as he wrote.

It was, indeed, me at the park today. I saw Edward's distress and could not resist helping him in a way that might solve future, similar problems. He will not get lost again, since he will not stop checking his direction. I am sure you will find it quite tiresome sometimes, as my mother did with me.

He chuckled at the memory.

As for Mrs Abbott,

He considered and rejected inventing an imaginary wife to solve the problem of her interest in him. For one thing, it would create as many problems as it solved. And for another, no matter how little sense it made, he did not want her to give up hope. If he could not manage to do so, why should she?

He continued.

> *I regret to inform you that no such lady exists. That makes our meeting an impossibility. I fear society would form the wrong impression should I spend too much time in your company.*

He bit his lip, considering how to explain in a way that would not hurt her feelings.

> *Much as we both might wish it to be otherwise, a visit between us is quite impossible. I am not the man you think me, my dear, and after the briefest of meetings, you would call an end to our friendship. I value that connection more than you can understand and am loath to spoil it a moment before its natural end.*
> *I speak of the day, coming soon, when you will re-enter society and find that worthy gentleman who will offer you a relationship based in flesh and blood rather than ink and paper. Then you will no longer need me and I will have to relinquish you to a better man.*
> *But until that day, I remain,*
> *Your Abbott*

He sighed as he sanded the wet ink, staring down at the letter in regret. The truth hurt him, but it was a thing he had ignored for far too long. He did not want to be the illusion that stood between her and true happiness, but, in a year of writing, that was just what he had become. And he could not imagine that her opinions had changed much on the worth of the Duke of Glenmoor.

In the distance, he heard the sound of the front door opening and closing and the bustle of servants greeting a guest. A few moments later, his brother appeared in the doorway of the study, causing him to slip the letter into the desk drawer to post later.

Evan was waving a letter of his own as he entered the room, holding it out with a flourish and dropping it on the centre of the empty desk. 'A missive from my wife. It seems we are to have a ball. If I cannot avoid it, neither can you. But we can at least save the postage by settling the matter of the invitation in person.'

'I will attend, of course,' Alex said, opening the invitation with a smile. 'As long as Maddie does not waste too much energy in matchmaking for me.'

'That, I cannot promise,' Evan said with a shake of his head. 'She has taken it into her mind that you should marry and be as happy as we are. So if there is anyone in particular you wish her to invite…'

The words hung in the air between them as Alex considered. Then he replied, 'Perhaps not for the reason she expects. Would it be too forward to request that Ogilvie's widow be invited?'

'Are you still obsessed about that?' Evan said, raising an eyebrow. 'It has been a year. The *ton* has moved on and you are all but forgiven.'

'Not by everyone,' Alex said, frowning as he thought of the dark looks he sometimes received when he entered a card room. 'There is still a faint pall hanging over my name in some circles. But it is not for my benefit that I wish you to invite her. The last year has been difficult for her.' He paused and added, 'Or so I suspect', since there should be no way he would know the truth.

'And you wish to give her what advantages you can, as you did with the invitation to my wife's Mathematical Society,' Evan concluded for him.

'It will do her good to be out in mixed company,' Alex agreed. 'Once she is married again, the scandal can truly be laid to rest.' And he would solve the problem he had created for her when he'd become Abbott.

'And what will happen when she realises that you are at this ball as well?' Alex asked, giving him a sceptical look.

If he was not careful, he would reveal his feelings by staring at her like a parched man near a glass of water. Even now, he felt a tickling excitement at the thought that they might soon be in the same room.

He forced it away and said, 'I do not know. For myself, I mean to make no trouble for her. I hope she will avoid me as well. Surely there will be other diversions to occupy her attention and other men who wish to speak to her?'

'That is probably true,' Evan agreed. 'I hear she is quite pretty.' Was he now looking at Alex with undue interest?

It did not matter. He could not help but answer honestly. 'Too beautiful to be a widow for long.'

'I see,' Evan replied. There was a pause before he added, 'And what of your plans for the future? Are there no other ladies you would like to see there?'

Alex gave a nervous laugh and shook his head. 'When there is someone, you will be the first to know. But at the present time there is no one with a claim on my heart.' At least no one he could reasonably offer for.

Evan gave an exasperated shake of his head. 'Very well, then. My wife will have to content herself with finding a match for Mrs Ogilvie. But do not think you can escape for another year. There will be no peace in my house until you are married.'

'Perhaps later in the Season,' he agreed. When Selina had married and he'd lost all reason to hope for the true happiness he imagined with her.

Chapter Four

It was Selina's first society ball.

When she had been young and unmarried, there had been no time or money for a London Season. Her father had said it was just so much nonsense and that a marriage could easily be arranged without it. Then he had died, as had her mother, and the point had been moot.

But he had been posthumously proven right when John Ogilvie had appeared in the neighbourhood to visit an old friend from school. It had taken little more than an introduction and a few meetings before he had offered for her, promising a glamorous future as mistress of a large London house.

It was not until they were married that she had discovered how precarious that life with him would be. Their house was fine enough, but not as grand as he'd described to her. Money that might have been spent on other entertainments was eaten up by her husband's vices. And the men John met in card rooms and gambling hells were not willing to invite him into their homes after emptying his purse.

But tonight, it would all be different.

As she was announced by the footman in the doorway of the Duke of Fallon's ballroom, she ran a hurried hand down her skirt, making sure that the moss green silk hung in even folds. Then she advanced into the room, smiling at the people who looked up to notice her arrival. She knew a few of the women from the Mathematical Society and offered a gracious thank you to the Duchess for thinking of her.

That woman responded with a mischievous smile of her own and pronounced herself happy to welcome her, now that her year of mourning was over. 'You cannot live in the past,' she said, gesturing out into the crowd on the dance floor. 'And there are many of us here who are eager to see you find your future.'

'Thank you,' Selina replied, wondering at the words. She suspected that *many* was an exaggeration, for none of those supposed friends had visited her after her husband's death and few had offered help in the months that followed. But she had one true advocate and she suspected he was behind this invitation.

The Duchess must know Abbott. But they were certainly not close enough for Selina to question her on the matter. She must hope that he revealed himself in some other way. He might be in the room with her even now. Perhaps this would be the night they met.

She smiled and looked around her, immediately catching the attention of Mary Wilson and some of the other women of her acquaintance. They hurried to introduce her to gentlemen and Selina was surprised to see her dance card filling with eager partners.

When only a few spaces remained, a shadow fell across the card. She looked up to find the Duke of Glenmoor standing beside her, staring down at it as if it was his business to do so. 'Mrs Ogilvie,' he said in a strangled tone, and offered her a stiff bow.

For a moment, she was too shocked to say anything at all. Then a host of rage-fuelled possibilities rushed to her lips. What right did he have to bother her after what he had done? Did he think that a bow and a quadrille would make up for the mess he had made in her life? Did he have to spoil the only evening she'd had out in a year?

Fortunately, her retorts stayed safely locked inside her as courtesy took the reins of her temper. She stared at him, for only a moment. Then she looked through him, offering nothing more than icy uninterest. If anyone in London deserved the cut direct, it was this man.

He shifted ever so slightly, trying to catch her eye. When it was clear that she did not plan to yield and recognise him, he murmured, 'Good evening', and moved away again.

When he was gone, she let out her held breath and heard the murmurs of gossip swirling about her, spreading like tendrils of fog through the room. Soon, everyone would know that a humble widow had cut a duke. It would likely be in the scandal sheets tomorrow. To court such notoriety would be either her making or her doom.

Then she heard a slow, soft clapping and Mr Baxter announced, 'Well done.'

If Glenmoor was the last man in London she wished to see, then Baxter was the second to the last. But she could not cut two men in a row. Even her friends would call her mad. So she offered him a chilly nod and made to walk away.

He stepped in front of her, blocking her path. 'So good to see you, Mrs Ogilvie, after so long.'

'Mr Baxter,' she said, then tried to move again.

'Is that an opening I see on your dance card? And for a waltz. You must not sit idle for that.' The card dangled from a ribbon on her wrist and he reached for her hand to take it.

'On the contrary,' she said, pulling away. 'It has been a long time since I have been out and I do not want to become overtaxed. But at the present, I am promised to another.' She smiled past him at the gentleman that had come to claim her for the first country dance.

Baxter stepped aside with an annoyed smile. 'We will talk later. But we will talk.'

Not if she could find a way to avoid it. For the moment, she was relieved to be able to occupy herself with dancing. One set followed another, which was followed by a glass of champagne and a visit to the buffet. After that, she spent some time conversing with friends. Before she'd realised, two hours had slipped by and she had forgotten all about him.

It was a delightful evening and she had not had such fun in well over a year. But by midnight, the room had become stuffy with the press of so many active people and she passed through the French doors along the back wall and out into the attached rose garden, seeking to cool herself in the night air.

But she was no sooner out of the house than Baxter came up behind her on the path, linking his arm in hers and walking at her side as if they were old friends.

She started, trying to pull away from him, but he held her fast and in a position of such casual intimacy that anyone observing would only remark on it if they saw her struggling to get away from him. If she wished to avoid more gossip, there was nothing to do but endure.

'Mrs Ogilvie,' he said with a note of triumph in his voice.

'What do you want from me?' she whispered, trying and failing to regain control of her arm.

'Only to get answers to a few simple questions.'

'Then ask them,' she said, giving him a frosty smile. 'And when you are through, leave me alone.'

'That I will not do,' he said softly. 'I have been thinking of you for over a year. And wondering how it is that you have managed to survive when you did not have a penny to your name after your husband died.'

'I received a bequest from an uncle,' she said, reciting the words that had been suggested to her by Abbott so long ago.

'How interesting,' he said, his fingers tightening on her arm. 'I was well acquainted with your husband before he died. When Ogilvie spoke of you, he was quite clear on the fact that he had married a woman with no family. You, my dear, are alone in the world. And yet you have managed to land on your feet, rent a home in a nice neighbourhood and secure an invitation to the Duke of Fallon's ball.'

'I am not alone,' she said, trying to keep the quaver out of her voice. It was a lie. Right now, when she needed help, she was very much alone and had no idea how to deal with this man.

'I am aware of that. And that brings me to my next question. Who is really helping you? And what were you willing to do to secure that help?'

She jerked her arm, trying to dislodge his grip. 'I did nothing untoward. It was an inheritance.'

'Do not lie to me,' he said softly. 'I will find out the truth, sooner or later.'

She had to fight to control her panic now. Her breath came in shallow gasps and she could feel her body beneath her gown slick with a cold sweat. Even if she told him the truth, Baxter would not believe it. The truth was far too unlikely to be believed. He would say she had given her favours to a man in exchange for security. It was what he was thinking, after all, and what he wanted for himself.

Then, before she could form an answer to his questions, his arm tensed against hers and she felt the jerk as he started in alarm, just as she had done when he'd grabbed her. When she glanced to her side, she saw a hand resting on Baxter's shoulder, the long white fingers sunk into the wool of his coat in a grip that must be painfully tight.

Then a voice came from just behind them. 'Baxter, isn't it?'

The man beside her nodded.

'The lady appears to be uncomfortable. Let her go.' There was a brief pause followed by the single word, 'Now.'

Baxter's arm slithered away from hers and he took a deliberate step to the side, away from her.

'Very good.' The hand on his shoulder gave a re-assuring pat. 'I suggest you give your regards to our hostess and say your goodbyes. It is either that or I will tell her that you are annoying one of her guests and have you removed from the premises.'

Baxter muttered a curse and said, 'This is not over.'

'I think it is,' said the man behind her.

There was a moment where she thought Baxter might be ready to argue. But the shadowed man behind them was large and as unyielding as a granite monument. So, with a final huff of irritation, Baxter retreated and the other stepped forward and took his place at her side.

He rested his hand gently on her arm and murmured, 'Come, Mrs Ogilvie. Let us take a seat while you regain your composure.'

'Glenmoor,' she said, staring up at him in horror as he guided her towards a bench set against the ivy-covered garden wall.

'I am not much of an improvement,' he said with a sympathetic smile. 'But needs must when the devil drives.'

'What did you hear?' she managed to say as she sank down on the seat.

'Nothing I care to repeat or remember,' he said, sitting down beside her. He stretched his legs out in front of him and adjusted his posture until he was near enough to her that she might feel the warmth of his presence, even though he was not touching her.

She tried not to lean into him, for after Baxter's threats there was a part of her longing to seek solace wherever she might find it. Things had been going so well. Now she felt as she had right after the funeral, when Baxter had paid his first visit, weak and vulnerable, wishing she could lay her head on someone's shoulder and cry.

She straightened, summoned all her resolve and leaned away from him. If she broke down now, she was likely to descend into uncontrollable hysterics, and she refused to do that in front of the man who'd ruined her life, no matter how annoyingly gallant his recent behaviour had been.

'This changes nothing between us,' she said, rising from the bench to get away from him.

'You're welcome,' he replied, remaining where he was. 'I recommend that you return to the ballroom, which is just up the path to your right.'

'I can find it myself,' she snapped. 'I don't need—'

'—a compass?' he concluded.

'Your help,' she corrected, giving him a final glare.

'Of course not,' he said, giving her a gesture of dismissal as she turned and hurried back to the house.

Chapter Five

At the Duke of Fallon's ball last night, witnesses
were treated to a most interesting sight. The
lovely Mrs O. met with the man who made her a
widow. The fairer sex might not be able to wield
a sword, but that did not prevent her from staring daggers at the Duke of G.

Alex sipped his breakfast coffee and stared down
at the gossip column in the morning paper, unsure
whether to be amused or frustrated. It was another
black mark on his smudged reputation. But at least a
point had been scored in favour of the brave widow
Ogilvie, who had stood up to him. People would
be looking for her at future events, eager to see the
woman brave enough to snub a duke.

Much as it had hurt to see her response to him, he
was proud of the way she had handled herself and the
way she had maintained composure, even in the face
of Baxter's pestering. He had watched her closely all
evening, counting the times she had danced and the

times she had sat out, making mental notes of the men who had paid her particular attention. It was almost as if he was launching a sister on her first Season.

At least, he had told himself that she should be like a sister. But when he had seen her standing in the entrance of the Fallon ballroom, stunning in a green gown that brought out the grey of her eyes, he had not felt the least bit fraternal. And seeing the dazed looks on the faces of the men around him, all clamouring for her attention, he had felt a most unbrotherly jealousy and the desire to pull her away from the crowd and keep her all to himself.

It had been stupid of him. For a moment, he had been thinking of all the fond letters that passed between them and imagining that, somehow, she knew that it was he who had written and understood that he meant no harm to her or her family. It was why he had approached her, unable to resist offering her a welcome back to society as his true self.

She had responded just as he'd known she would, with contempt and disdain. Before they had parted, he had not been able to resist a final hint at the truth and mentioned the compass, smiling at her and hoping to see some glimmer of recognition in her eyes.

It had fallen flat. What could he do to get her to see past her hatred of him, even for a moment? And why did he want to? It was not as if she would fall into his arms once she discovered he was Abbott. She might loathe him even more for his intrusion into her life.

But for a little while longer, he could still be Abbott for her, that undemanding paragon who was worthy

of her regard. As he expected, there was a letter from
her in the afternoon post, asking his advice.

I thank you, dear Abbott, for arranging the invi-
tation, but fear that I have managed things very
badly. I've got my name in the papers over the
way I handled meeting that odious Glenmoor.

Alex winced. If he was still odious, he had been
foolish to hope for forgiveness or to imagine that there
could be anything more between them. He read on.

And now I have Mr Baxter to contend with
as well. He insists that he will discover the
source of my support, which cannot be good
news for either one of us. Since you have re-
mained anonymous thus far, I assume that you
have your reasons for secrecy. I will understand
if the threat of discovery makes you rethink our
arrangement.

It should. It really should. A sane man would find
a way to give her up. He got out his plain paper and
crafted an answer.

My dear Mrs Ogilvie,
Do not worry yourself about the appearance of
Baxter and his threats. We will find a way to
defeat him together.

Lord knew what that was. But there must be something he could do that would decrease the scandal rather than making it worse.

And do not think for a moment that I would leave you in your hour of need, or run from idle threats, especially coming from a grubby little nothing like Baxter.

And what was he to say about the odious Glenmoor? What could he say? He decided to ignore the insult and move on to happier things.

For now, you must focus on the obvious successes of the evening. You look stunning in green. You were very popular and danced frequently. Surely you took some pleasure in that? There will be other invitations, I am sure, and events that have no clouds hanging over them.
Until then, know that I am,
Your devoted Abbott

Satisfied, he blotted, sealed and set the letter with the outgoing mail.

Selina rushed to the door when the next morning's post arrived, half dreading the response she knew would be there. She had done the right thing in offering Abbott a way out of their arrangement, for it was not fair to drag a good man down with her, should she fall from grace.

But all the same, she prayed that he would refuse

her suggestion. She wanted him. She needed him. She could not imagine a life without him, even though he insisted one must soon come. The men she'd met at the Fallon ball had all been charming enough. All equally well-mannered and attentive, and all but one had been good dancers. But in the day and a half that had passed, the memories of them seemed blurry and unimportant compared to Glenmoor and Baxter and the shadowy presence of the man who wrote the letter she was about to read.

She scanned it quickly, taking in his vow of loyalty with a sigh of relief and his promise that they would best her nemesis somehow.

Then her eyes caught on a single line and she shook the paper as she would shake Abbott were he to appear before her right now.

You look stunning in green.

He had been there. He had been in the same room with her, perhaps even danced with her or spoken to her without giving himself away.

How else would he have known the colour of her dress, or how much she had danced?

But had he seen Baxter harassing her? Obviously not or it would have been Abbott that came to her rescue and not the Duke. He would not have left her unguarded, would he? She tried to remember the men that had been in the garden when the incident had happened, but when Baxter had laid his hand on her arm, her mind had gone blank.

And after Glenmoor was through with her, she had fled for home, unable to stand another moment. Even now, the thought of the man aroused a strange mingling of hatred and curiosity. He had removed Baxter from her presence as if he was flicking a fly from her sleeve. Then he'd sat down next to her and behaved in a way he probably thought was comforting.

In truth, it had been more unnerving than anything else. It had been hard enough to stand up to him in a crowded ballroom. But alone in the dark she was aware of the size of him, the sheer masculine power and the same confidence that he had used to dispense with Baxter.

She shook her head, trying to relieve herself of the memory. She would do as Abbott had said and think of the rest of the ball, and the fact that he had been there. That was all that mattered. She hugged the paper to her heart, her problems momentarily forgotten.

She decided that they had danced, because, if she was to have a fantasy, it must be the best one possible. Their conversation had been banal and forgettable, but all the while he had been laughing to himself at the trick he was playing on her and admiring the way she looked in candlelight.

And he had held her in his arms.

That was a lie, she was sure. She had not danced the waltz, for she had not been prepared for the intimacy of such a dance with men she had just met. But in her imagination, she waltzed with Abbott, laughing and spinning and dipping.

And if she had not? Then perhaps at the next ball, or the next. He was out there, moving through the *ton* like a fish in water. She had but to find him and allow him to win her. Then they would be together just as she hoped and everything about her life would come right.

Chapter Six

'What do you know about a man named Bernard Baxter?' Alex was sitting in his brother's study in the Fallon townhouse, enjoying an afternoon brandy.

Evan's brow furrowed. 'When we were at school together, he was an evil little toady.'

'Then what was he doing at your ball the other night?' Alex asked, honestly curious.

'Because he is as lucky at cards as John Ogilvie was unlucky. Half of London owes him money and the other half owe him a favour.'

'And you?'

'I invited him as a guest of Lord and Lady Ellerby, who fall into one of those two categories,' Evan said, refilling his drink. 'Why the sudden interest in him?'

Alex frowned. 'I was surprised that he was there. I caught him bothering a friend of mine and threatened to put him out.'

'A lady friend?' Evan said with a sly smile.

'That is of no importance,' Alex said hurriedly. 'I

was simply surprised that Baxter would be among your guests.'

'You will not see him here again, if that is really your concern. He has no strings on me, nor will he ride into my house on someone's coat-tails, now that I have heard he was causing trouble.'

'That is good to know,' Alex said. He still had no clue as to what to do about the man, but at least his assessment of the fellow's character was correct.

'Now tell me more about your female friend,' Evan said, leaning forward expectantly. 'Is she, perhaps, above stairs right now, attending my wife's Mathematical Society?'

'Why would you think so?' Alex said. It was not quite a denial; therefore, it was not a lie.

'It is not unusual for you to visit here, but it is co-incidental that you convinced me to come back here during the meeting. Normally, I avoid the house when it is packed with my wife's friends and do my drinking at White's.'

'I did not want to discuss Baxter in public,' Alex said, any more than he wanted to discuss Selina in private.

But it did not appear that Evan was ready to let the matter drop. 'If you really have no favourite, you will find any number of eligible young ladies attend my wife's salons,' he said. 'And, occasionally, gentlemen, if they are interested in mathematics.'

'Or young ladies,' Alex said, setting down his glass and backing towards the hall, which already held a stream of departing females. 'But since all I wanted was information, I will be on my way.'

Selina sat towards the back of the room in the crowded nursery of the Fallon townhouse, a notebook in front of her, dutifully scratching the examples on the pages and struggling to understand the equation that the Duchess had chalked on to the blackboard in front of them.

The usual occupant of the nursery, little Frederick, was in the corner of the room with his nurse, chewing on an amber teething bracelet and staring at his mother with the same confusion that Selina felt.

She had no passion for mathematics, as some of the women in the room did, and was often confused by the puzzles and enigmas in the *Ladies' Digest*. But she had to admit that the biscuits and teacakes served here were better than her cook made at home and the conversation with the other ladies was excellent. She smiled at Mary, who occupied the seat on her left, and glanced at the clock, just as the Duchess of Fallon announced an end to the lesson for the day.

All around her, notebooks shut with snaps and, in the front, she heard a few disappointed sighs. But then the footman distributed tea and petits fours and the work was forgotten.

An hour later, the women thanked the Duchess and dispersed.

'I love these gatherings,' Mary said enthusiastically, then whispered, 'And I do not mind catching a glimpse of the Duke as well. The man is quite handsome, don't you think?'

Selina offered a 'Shh' and looked around to see if they had been overheard. 'You are married and so is he, if I need to remind you.'

Mary laughed and nudged her playfully in the arm. 'I am well aware of the fact. But it does no harm to look. In my opinion, you do far too little of that. Was there not someone from the ball that you would not mind seeing again?'

'From the ball?' she said with a blush. They were headed down the stairs towards the ground floor now.

'Someone other than your mysterious friend,' Mary clarified, her hand skimming the marble banister. 'If he has not come forward in a year, it is probably not wise to favour him with your full attention. If you choose another champion, he will either go away or be shaken loose from his reticence.'

The former was exactly what she'd feared would happen. That was why it was so difficult to focus her attention on other men. She did not want to risk losing Abbott.

'I met no one in particular,' she said at last. At least not anyone that she had wanted to see again. Baxter had been all too eager to see her and she dreaded his next appearance. 'But it is early in the Season and I have only been to one gathering. And there are hundreds of men in London. And…'

And one was right in front of her at the foot of the steps, oblivious to the women passing behind him. The Duke of Glenmoor stood, back to the chattering crowd, talking to someone down the hall and out of sight. It was probably the Duke of Fallon, for everyone knew they were as close as blood brothers and often seen together.

Why, of all people, did it have to be him?

Selina hesitated for a moment, unsure of how to get past without being noticed. Then she composed herself and continued down the stairs. She would simply walk, head held high, and do her best to ignore him. If she did not call attention to herself, he might never notice her.

Of course, given her luck, that was a desperate plan that could not possibly succeed. As she reached Glenmoor's side, he turned and stepped directly into her path and she ran into him.

He was solid in a masculine way that she wished she could ignore. And so very tall. And he smelled of sandalwood with a fresh green scent of soap underneath.

Her breath left her in a relieved sigh as if her body recognised, though her mind did not want to, that it had been a long time since she had been this close to a man, even closer than dancing. His hand came out immediately to steady her and the touch on her arm tingled.

For a moment, he seemed as shocked as she was. Then he said, 'Mrs Ogilvie.' And nothing else, as if the impact of their bodies had knocked the sense out of him.

'Your Grace.' She must be senseless as well for she could not even manage her usual indignation.

'I beg your pardon.'

They said it together, apologising in a choral unison that would have made two other people laugh in shared recognition of the absurdity.

Instead, there was an embarrassing pause, as each waited for the other to speak, or at least to move.

Then the Duke said, 'A lovely day we're having.' He paused again, as if noticing that they were not outside and that it was cloudy and spitting rain, so the conversational opening was wrong. He tried again. 'You were at the Mathematical Society, I suppose.'

She nodded, still too shocked to draw her arm out of his grasp.

'I was visiting with Fallon,' he said, stating the obvious. Then he turned, remembering his manners, and his hand slipped away. 'And this is your friend, I suppose.' He waited for an introduction.

She had forgotten that she had no intention of speaking to this man. She should snub him again and walk out the door and into the rain without looking back.

But before she could manage it, Mary elbowed her in the ribs to force more words out of her.

'Mrs Mary Wilson, may I introduce the Duke of Glenmoor.'

'Your Grace.'

'Charmed.' He bent over Mary's hand. Then he straightened and gave her a smile that made her giggle almost as much as she had at the thought of Fallon. 'May I offer the two of you a ride to make up for this inconvenience I have caused?'

'No.'

'Yes, thank you.'

This time, she spoke in unison with Mary, who drowned her out, leaving her refusal ignored, as the Duke signalled a footman to call for his carriage to take them home.

It was nothing, really. It meant nothing. But if that was true, why could she still not catch her breath? It was probably her smothered anger at his presence that was causing this upheaval. Her every muscle tensed as he handed her up into a seat, and she sat in silence as he made polite conversation with Mary, asking after her husband, her children and her interest in the Duchess of Fallon's latest enigma.

Was he flirting with her? It would be just like him to seduce someone else's wife. Was that better or worse than setting his sights upon an unmarried girl and offering her unchaperoned rides? Selina was not sure. And it was not as if the two of them were alone now. Selina was here as a third, if one was needed.

Mary responded, hesitantly at first, then with more enthusiasm, chatting amicably until the carriage rolled to a stop in front of Selina's home.

This was the moment where she ought to thank him for his consideration. But the words stuck in her throat. He must know she wanted none of his help. But if that were true, why hadn't she refused the ride and left Mary to her own devices?

She got out of the carriage, leaving her friend alone with the Duke as the horses started off again. Selina stared at their retreat, wondering what had just occurred. The peer had been doing his best to appear ordinary and non-threatening. It was obvious that he had won Mary over with a few kind words and a seat in his carriage.

But it would take more than that to convince Selina, especially after the uneasy way she felt whenever she was close to him. No one who aroused such strangeness in her could be trusted. It would explain his moment of awkwardness as well, for he'd needed a moment of preparation to put on a false and friendly face for her.

But what was his purpose with Mary? Had he made a point of taking her home last, specifically so that he could be alone with her? She was married, of course, and should be off-limits to predation. Was the man devoid of honour, or had it been an innocent courtesy? She must write to Abbott, tell him of these latest developments and ask his opinion.

The next letter from Selina arrived as Alex was sitting down to supper and he took it into the dining room with him, unable to wait until after the meal to read it.

The afternoon had been both a catastrophe and a triumph. After an unconvincing attempt to justify his presence in the house to Evan, he had literally run into Selina in the front hall. He hoped his brother had not heard him stammering about the weather like some awkward schoolboy smitten by his first love. If so, he would never hear the end of it.

As usual, she showed no desire to talk with him. Luckily, her friend was in awe of his title and had been desperate to prolong the conversation. It had given him an excuse to offer them a ride.

He'd sat across from them in the carriage, so he might stare at Selina at leisure while carrying on a conversation with her friend. She had been wearing a gown of soft rose that gave her complexion a healthy glow and made her eyes shine like moonlight. But she'd stayed prim and silent for the whole of the trip and he had dropped her off first, not wanting to press his already thin luck.

When she was gone, he had enquired gently after her, admitting that he did not think Mrs Ogilvie had enjoyed herself, but thanking Mrs Wilson for allowing him to assist them.

'I am sure that is not the case,' the woman had said, lying to save his feelings. 'She was complaining of a megrim before we ran into you. But it was most gracious of you to offer to drive us home. It saved us from having to walk in the rain. I doubt she is so stubborn to allow herself a soaking rather than a ride in a fine carriage such as this.'

And then, the conversation had turned to the weather, and he had learned nothing more. But surely this letter would give him insight. He popped the seal and scanned the contents as he started on his soup.

His spoon froze halfway to his mouth, then clattered back.

I could not avoid another interaction with that horrible Glenmoor...
He drove us home from Fallon House and he

*would not stop talking to my friend Mrs Wilson.
He showed no respect for her married state and
flirted most shamelessly with her for the whole
of the ride.*

She thought he was angling after Mary Wilson.
What had he done to imply that? Did she think him
incapable of common courtesy? Apparently, he was
a villain through and through.

He re-read the passage describing their meeting,
where she described him as *lying in wait in the hallway.*

Perhaps that had a note of truth in it. He had known
that she would be there, with the rest of the ladies for
the Mathematical Society. And he had timed his exit
from Evan's study to occur when they were leaving,
hoping to catch a glimpse of her.

But walking into her had been an accident. He was
sure. Or almost so. There had been nothing preda-
tory about it. And he had only spoken to her friend
because that woman had been willing to converse.
It had made for a handy excuse to spend a few moments with Selina.

But to think he had designs on Mary? She was
clearly married. He was not about to seduce her. He
crumpled the letter in one fist and slammed the other
on the table, making the china jump in response.

Behind him, a footman shifted nervously, probably wondering if there was something wrong with
his meal.

Alex took a deep breath to calm himself. Then he

deliberately folded the letter and slipped it into his pocket, eating mechanically as he formed a response in his mind. He waited a full five minutes after pudding before taking his port to the study and sharpening a quill.

> *Mrs Ogilvie,*
> *I am sorry to hear of your trying afternoon and hope that it has not put you off attending the Duchess's little meetings, as I know how much you have enjoyed them in the past. I would hate to hear that you avoid the Fallon house in the future, just because of a chance encounter.*
> *As for Glenmoor, and his attentions to your friend, I am sure he meant nothing by them and that she is far too sensible to have her head turned by a few kind words, even if they come from a duke. Do not think so little of her, even if you cannot think well of him.*

There. He smiled and nodded in satisfaction. It did not precisely redeem his attempt to meet her, but perhaps it minimised the damage.

He paused and dipped his quill again, staring at the blank space left to fill. There had to be something he could do to soften her feelings towards him. Perhaps the admirable Mr Abbott could spare him a kind word or two.

> *Personally, I pity the gentleman. I think it is far more likely that Glenmoor behaves strangely*

*because he is stunned by your beauty and loses
all sense when he is around you.*

*You are likely shaking your head at the idea,
but that is only because you underestimate the
effect you have on the gentlemen around you.
When it comes to matters of the heart, peers
are no different than other men, susceptible to
beauty. And yours is such a unique loveliness
paired with such a charming nature that I am
sure he is quite overcome by you.*

He signed, blotted and sealed the letter, then walked
to the hall to set it with the outgoing post. Now he had
but to wait to see her response to the suggestion that
the Duke, whom she held in such low esteem, might
be utterly besotted with her. His letter might do nothing to minimise her hatred for him and her general
distrust of every overture he made, but at least he had
admitted the truth.

Selina stared down at the latest letter from Abbott,
deeply unsatisfied with his answer. It seemed to her
that he gave too much credit to the Duke and too little
to her suspicions of his character.

But then she re-read the last paragraph and read
it one more time, smiling. He thought her handsome.
No, more than that, if he thought she was the sort of
woman to render a man insensible in person.

The motives that he attributed to the Duke were
clearly his own. It was another tentative proof that

he shared the attraction she felt for him, a love that he seemed to think could never be consummated.

Perhaps this explained why he only communicated by writing. He was too intimidated to meet her in person. It was ridiculous, of course. She had been married for eight years and had heard no such compliments from John, nor had he been awed by his good luck in catching her. She could not even muster enough allure to keep him at home.

But, apparently, Abbott was a different sort of man. What could she say to encourage him to overcome his shyness and meet with her? Whatever the words, they must not be sent in a letter, for it only reinforced the idea that she was unreachable. They must meet in person and she could think of one place to look.

Chapter Seven

It was a week to the moment since Edward had come to her with the compass and Selina was back in the park, pacing nervously on the path. Today, she had forgone the company of both friend and son and come alone for her walk. It was probably a vain hope. But perhaps Abbott kept regular habits and walked at this time each day, or each week. In case it was not his plan, she had hinted in her last letter to him that this was her usual time for a walk. Maybe he would come to watch for her.

If he was here, he might gather his nerve and talk to her. Or perhaps she would catch sight of a familiar face and be able to guess the identity of the man who so intrigued her.

But it seemed it was not to be. She could not see anyone who seemed the least bit interesting, nor did anyone seem to be interested in her. And she did not want to stare at strangers, lest she draw the sort of inappropriate attention that she was getting from Baxter.

It had been a mistake to come out here at all. She was making a fool of herself over a man who had made no promises. A few guarded compliments were nothing to build a future on. She dropped down on the nearest bench, overcome with defeat.

Then she saw someone she did know and it made her feel even worse. Baxter was heading down the path towards her at a pace that was almost a trot. For a moment, she had the terrible idea that he had been Abbott all the time and had used the letters as a way to get close to her.

But that could not be right. He'd have used the money against her by now or gained some advantage by all the insight she had given him into her life and her mind. The fact that he was in a public park with her was merely an unfortunate coincidence.

Her legs tensed as she considered rising, then rejected it. To get up and move away she would have to run from him. And there were no shadows and moonlight to hide what was happening. All would see her and note the interaction and she would be back in the scandal sheets again. It would be better to hold her place and hold her tongue, waiting for him to give up and leave her alone.

But before he could reach her, Glenmoor dropped into the seat at her side, offering a smile and a nod. 'Mrs Ogilvie, how are you today?'

Why was the man everywhere that she wanted to be? And why would he not leave her alone? As usual, he was the epitome of elegance in a blue coat, buff breeches and tasselled Hessians that gleamed in the sunlight. 'Your Grace,' she said, deliberately jerking her skirts away from where they settled against his leg. Then she looked straight ahead, refusing to meet his gaze or acknowledge his question.

As usual, her rudeness did not seem to bother him. 'I know that the situation is not ideal. You do not want my company. But then I doubt you wanted Baxter's company either. It is a difficult choice, is it not? So, I have made it for you.'

There was the hint of a breeze and the scent of his cologne reached her, mysterious and seductive, making it even harder to pretend he was not there. Why did such an awful person have to smell so thoroughly inviting? 'Go away,' she murmured, still staring straight ahead and trying not to breathe.

Oblivious as always, he sighed and stretched out his legs, settling in rather than offering to move. 'I do not think that is a good idea. Let us just sit here and enjoy the view together, shall we?'

She gave up and turned to acknowledge him with a glare. 'I will find it more enjoyable once you are gone.'

'And then Baxter will take my seat and insult you,' he reminded her in a pleasant voice. 'And you will have no good way to rid yourself of him. Better that he has to fight his way through me. I doubt he will bother, as it is exceptionally bad form to argue with a peer.' He gave her a sidelong look. 'You should learn that as well, I think.'

She sucked in her breath through her teeth. 'I did not seek you out. I go out of my way to avoid you.

And there is nothing that you can do to earn my forgiveness.'

'Not for want of trying,' he said in the same mild tone.

Was that what he was doing by trapping her like this? Trying to gain some absolution? If so, it would not work. What he had done was beyond forgiveness. But that did not mean that she could forgo his help at the moment. She sighed in resignation and watched as Baxter approached. Glenmoor was right. He did not dare leave her now. 'You are the lesser of two evils,' she agreed.

This seemed to amuse the Duke, who let out a small laugh. 'I knew you would see it my way.'

Baxter had reached them now and paused in front of the bench, staring from her to the Duke and back as if expecting Glenmoor to yield his position.

The Duke stared placidly back at him and did not move an inch. 'Mr Baxter? Is there something I can help you with?'

For a moment, she thought he would slink away without another word. Then he rallied and said, 'I wish to speak with Mrs Ogilvie.'

'She does not wish to speak to you,' the Duke replied.

For a moment, she was tempted to argue that he had no right to speak for her. But she was at a loss as to how to get rid of Baxter on her own, so she remained silent.

'She does not want to speak to you either,' Baxter said with a triumphant smile.

'But I, at least, am a gentleman,' Glenmoor responded. 'I am content to remain silent and not make any overtures that would offend her. If the same can be said of you, then you will have no problem conversing with her while I am present.'

Baxter let out a low growl and stared between them, unsure of what to do next.

'You might as well move along,' the Duke said, giving him his answer. 'I will not yield, if that is what you are expecting. And Mrs Ogilvie will not send me away to make space for you.'

Baxter shifted from foot to foot, obviously annoyed. Then he said, 'You will not always be here, Glenmoor.'

'Perhaps not. But I am here now and that is enough.'

Baxter looked to her now, as if she would stand up for him and send the Duke away so they could be together. It was time that she spoke for herself. 'Whatever the question, the answer is no. The next time you find me, the answer will still be no. The answer will always be no to whatever you want from me. Go away.' She followed this with her sternest look, holding her breath and hoping it would finally convince him to leave her alone.

He took a step back, as if the force of her rejection had driven him off balance. Then he caught himself again and said, 'I will leave you. For now. But I will be back and we *will* talk. Whatever you are doing to stay afloat without a husband, you cannot keep it up forever. When your plan fails, I will be there.' He gave her a final look, a gaze of pure avaricious desire. Then he walked off down the path as if nothing had happened.

For a moment, she could not breathe at all. There was no reason to believe that Abbott would leave her to this man's machinations. But Baxter had been so certain that she could not help her doubts.

The Duke sensed the silence and filled it. 'It is nothing more than empty talk. He wants to frighten you.'

'He succeeded,' she said, then added a laugh, trying to show a confidence she did not feel.

'You must never forget that you have the support of your friends,' he said, then added awkwardly, 'And me, of course.'

'Why?' Though she did not want to encourage the man, she could not stop the question from escaping and the nagging memory of Abbott's letter and his assumptions about the Duke's motives.

'I do not like bullies,' he said, staring down the path after Baxter and frowning. Then he looked back at her and smiled. 'And if you need help avoiding that one, I am at your service.'

'Your help will not be necessary,' she said, trying to gain control of a situation that had got quite out of hand.

His smile turned ironic. 'Of course not.'

'I am going home now,' she added, rising and heading towards the entrance to the park.

'I will give you a ride,' he said.

'It is not far. I mean to walk.'

'Then I will walk with you,' he said, refusing to take the hint.

She sighed. 'I cannot prevent you.' Then she set out, taking care not to glance to her side where he was keeping pace. Behind them, she heard the clatter of his carriage, following them in case he changed his mind and decided to ride. It felt as if she had wandered into a parade and somehow become the leader. She quickened her pace and he did as well. Behind her the harnesses jingled and the coach horses walked faster.

She stopped suddenly and he stopped as well, looking at her expectantly as she blurted, 'This is unbearable.'

He gestured back to the carriage. 'We could always—'

'No!' She glanced around her in all directions and said, 'Baxter is not following. We are alone. There is nothing wrong with the neighbourhood. No one is bothering me, except you.' She followed this with a withering stare, hoping to dent his confidence.

He blinked at her, unmoving.

She waved her hands at him in a shooing gesture. 'Go away. I am fine without you. I do not need you.'

'I do not think that is entirely true,' he said, pausing to wet his lips, and inhaled, as if there was something important that he needed to say.

If he was about to lecture her about her problems with Baxter, she did not wish to be reminded of them. And she certainly did not want to hear an offer of any other sort. What was she to do if Abbott was right and the man had romance on his mind?

'You have helped me enough for the day,' she interrupted. 'Now, I wish to be alone.'

He let out the preparatory breath he had taken, obviously deflated. Then, as if he could not take no for an answer, he added, 'If you are sure.'

'Very,' she said, pointing to the carriage.

'Good day, then.' He offered a deep bow and turned to his carriage, not looking back. A footman hopped down from it to get the door and he disappeared into the body. The door slammed, the footman hopped back into his seat and the vehicle set off, turning at the next corner.

She watched it until it was out of sight, then set off on her way again, hurrying to get home. Even after the door of her house was safely closed and locked, she was still shaken from her latest interaction with her two adversaries and unsure of what was to happen next. But there was one thing she could do now, the thing that she always did with each new change in her life.

She went to the desk, sharpened a quill and began to write.

Dear Abbott,
Baxter found me in the park today and tried to insinuate himself into my day. And once again, it was only the intervention of the Duke of Glenmoor that saved me from his company.

I am well aware of what Baxter wants from me. He has been bold enough to say it directly. The Duke is another matter. His intentions are murkier and he has not yet made them clear. But it is only a matter of time until he issues his proposition, which I will, of course, refuse.

*What am I to do if these men will not take
no for an answer?*

She closed the letter, sanded and sealed it, then sent
it out with the afternoon post, instructing her housekeeper that she was not at home, especially not to any
supposed gentlemen that might call.

After Selina dismissed him, Alex rode the rest of the
way to his home, relieved to be alone in his embarrassment. He had gone to the park during her usual walking time, hoping to catch a glimpse of her. He had not
been prepared to speak with her. And as usual, he had
managed it badly.

It was easiest to play the hero when he had Baxter to deal with. Baxter was inherently unlikable and
Alex could not resist goading him. Aside from that,
opposing him created a reason to speak with Selina
and things to say. He enjoyed protecting her. It felt
right, somehow.

But once the little toady was gone, she had been
eager to get rid of Alex and they'd fallen back into the
awkward silence that was a hallmark of their interactions.

Or at least, he had. She had been most loquacious,
and her chosen topic had been how much she wished
that he would go away. There had been a moment when
he had nearly confided the truth to her. He'd gathered
his nerve to the sticking point and was searching for
the right way to begin when she'd cut him off, with a

disavowal so firm there was no gentlemanly way to ignore it.

She'd continued in the same vein in her next letter to Abbott and he grimaced as he read her attributing Baxter's motives to him when he was entirely innocent.

As he sat down to write his response, he was tempted to remind her of her words on the street and tell her that the only reason she had managed at all was because of the Duke's help. But that would be petty and unfair.

He did not mind helping her and would continue to do so as long as he was able. But it was impractical to be Abbott when dealing with Baxter, and Glenmoor could not follow her everywhere, imposing himself on her and demanding that she accept his help. There was only one thing he could think of to do.

He began,

My dear Selina,
Do not worry yourself about Baxter. As I promised, a solution is at hand.

I am sending you a new servant, a footman of prodigious size, who may guard your door by day and follow you about on errands, if you so choose. He will be instructed as to Baxter's unwelcomeness and will escort the man off the premises should he try to call on you when you are at home.

As for the Duke, it is possible that he dislikes Baxter even more than you do and is following that man about for some reason that has noth-

*ing to do with you. Perhaps that is why he seems
ever present in your life. But...*

Alex paused, forming his words carefully. She
needed looking after and Glenmoor was in an excellent position to do so. He was a duke in need of an
heir. He would have to marry, eventually.

Why could it not be her?

If he could come to her as himself, he might never
need to reveal his deception as Abbott. Or at least
he could wait until so much later that it was nothing more than an amusing anecdote and not a fresh
source of betrayal.

*...it is also quite natural that he would be
interested in you. Unlike Baxter, I have heard
Glenmoor is a decent man and not likely to
make unseemly requests to a lady who has been
a guest in his brother's house.*

*Have you considered that his attraction to
you may be an honourable one? He is, after all,
unmarried and must seek a wife sooner rather
than later. I can think of no reason he would
not be drawn to someone as fine, as charming
and as noble as you.*

He smiled, warming to the idea. He could imagine
her beside him in bed, soft skin and smooth hair, the
scent of her, like spring flowers after a rain. He would
be the happiest of men.

And there would be advantages to her as well.

> *Baxter would not dare touch the wife of such*
> *a powerful man. And you would have power in*
> *your own right. You would be a duchess in a*
> *great house, dressed in silks and jewels, with*
> *servants to wait on your every need.*

The idea was insane. But it was the best solution, the happiest outcome for both of them. If only he could make her see.

He finished the letter quickly, sealing it before he could change his mind and retract the offer she would not know he was making. Then he put it in the outgoing post and sat back to wait.

Clearly, Abbott had gone mad. Selina stared down at the paper in her hand, re-reading it carefully to make sure she had understood correctly, for he was suggesting the unsuggestable.

Of course, he had begun with her Christian name, which was endearing, and extolled her virtues as a woman and wife. But no amount of flattery would make up for the fact that he wanted to give her away to the abominable Duke.

She ran to the morning room writing desk and took up her pen.

> *My dear Abbott,*
> *First, I must thank you for the offer of a foot-*
> *man, which does seem like a good temporary*
> *solution for these incursions into my life.*
> *   But as for the rest...*

*Even if I believed that the Duke's intentions
were honourable, there is no way I would consider a marriage to him. Have you forgotten
the role he played in the death of my husband?
The idea that I could link myself to such a man
is unfathomable. Even sitting next to him for
short periods of time is enough to make my
skin crawl.*

She paused for a moment, tempted to strike the last
line and write something else. Her interactions with
the Duke had indeed raised strange sensations in her,
though they were not quite as she had just described
them. But she was not sure how to chronicle the con-
flicting emotions she felt when looking at him, especially not to Abbott. She certainly did not want to give
the impression that she had taken a physical interest
in the man.

Though there was nothing particularly unnatural
about such an awareness. He was handsome, after
all. And she had been alone for a long time. But it
did not signify.

She shook her head, trying to clear it of wayward
thoughts, and continued her letter.

*He is the last man on earth I would marry,
even if he should offer.*
*Please, if you must make suggestions for my
future, come up with something better than that.*

Then, to remind him of the better thing she hoped for, she closed with

Yours, always, Selina

What had he expected?

Alex stared down at the letter, particularly the lines that described her reaction to him, remembering the expression of suspicion and loathing on her face each time they met. Her assumptions about her husband's last night were unchanged, even after a year.

In the few times they'd talked since, they'd exchanged only a handful of words, mostly about Baxter. He had never managed anything near to an explanation or an apology, or an assurance that she was mistaken about his part in any of it.

Unless things changed drastically in the future, there was no chance that he would earn her friendship, or even ambivalence. The idea of gaining her love was far beyond the realm of possibility.

He sighed. His wants were not part of this equation. She had asked him what she was to do about Baxter. There was one, easy solution that would make the man give up and go away. She needed someone who could protect her, not just occasionally, but always.

That man would not be him. He could not have her for himself no matter what he wanted. Nor could he expect her to stay a widow for the rest of her life. She was a flesh-and-blood woman who had needs.

At least, he assumed she did. When she wrote to

him, she seemed so full of life and passion. It was a crime against the universe that she should live with an empty bed and only a few tepid letters for company.

He took her latest letter to his study and sat down at his desk to pen his answer.

> *My dear Selina,*
> *It is clear that my first idea met with a poor reception. Forgive my impertinence for the suggestion. I only want what is best for you and that is to see you placed in society at a rank that suits you.*
>
> *But I am afraid the only true solution I have found to your problems is that you marry someone suitable who can care for you in ways that I cannot.*
>
> *That should be your ultimate goal, should it not? To find a husband who might keep you company and who would be a good father for your son. May I suggest a few gentlemen you are sure to meet, if you are invited to the Duchess of Melton's ball next week?*

He paused.

After an hour, he was still staring at a blank sheet, at a loss.

Evan would have been perfect had he not married. He was unequalled in character and good sense, just the sort of man Alex wanted for her. Perhaps it would be better to choose someone who was already a widower, with an heir who could be company for Edward. As long as the man was better than his own stepfather had been. He did not want to sentence the boy to a childhood like his own.

But that was not enough. The perfect husband must not gamble too much or drink too much. He must be healthy in mind and body. He must be attentive to her in all the ways John Ogilvie had not been. He must have enough money for her to live comfortably and enough sense to plan for the future so that she might never be thrown back into poverty.

He sat with his pen poised over the paper as he rejected name after name as unworthy, finally settling on three fellows in whom he could find no obvious flaws. He scribbled their names down, then signed and sealed the letter before he could change his mind.

Then he reached for the brandy bottle to numb the pain that would accompany the impending loss of the woman he could not help but love.

Chapter Eight

How dared he?

Selina crumpled the letter with frustration and headed towards the fire, ready to rid herself of it for good. At the last minute, she changed her mind and carried it back to the writing desk to read again.

It was one thing to suggest the Duke as a possible husband. He could not have been serious when he'd written that, knowing how she felt about Glenmoor. She had decided that it must have been meant as a joke between friends, though one that was not very funny. And it had been a little flattering to know that he thought her worthy of being a duchess, even if it linked her with a man she could not abide.

But this latest letter was serious and reasonable. Too reasonable. Logical to the point of coldness. Did he really mean to organise her future without a thought as to where her heart might lie? To suggest that she would marry one of these strangers and let that man take his place in her life as lover and protector? It was impossible.

She wrote back.

Do not say that this is the only way. Of course I would like to marry again. Sometime in the future. But I would rather face a dozen Baxters than marry without love.

She sent the brief missive off and waited for his response.

And waited.

When two days had passed, she wrote again.

I hope I have not offended you with my hasty words. It is unfair of me to imply that I am avoiding marriage for any reason. The alternative is to live on your charity and I realise I cannot do that the whole of my life. It was the height of selfishness to reject your suggestions out of hand.

If you wish to rethink your generosity, please tell me honestly and I will find another way to support myself.

Just the thought of that sent a chill through her, for she had no idea what she would do without him. But there were things far more important than money, his continued friendship foremost among them.

* * *

When another two days had passed with no word, she wrote again.

> *My dearest Abbott,*
> *What has become of you? I have never gone so long without a letter and you have me worried. Was it something I said? If so, I retract it and apologise.*
> *If it is just a matter of those gentlemen you suggested, I will dance with them at the ball tomorrow night and do my best to befriend them. We shall see what comes of it.*
> *But do not cut me out of your life without explanation. Just a line or two to assure me that you are not angry. Or something far worse.*
> *My mind runs wild with dire possibilities. If you are ill, tell me where I might go to tend you. I fear you are hurt and alone, or perhaps dead and beyond my reach forever. What shall I do if that is the case? Cannot someone answer me so I might lay a wreath and offer my prayers?*

Her fears were probably ridiculous, as were the tears she was shedding as she wrote the last words. It was much more likely that he had grown tired of their correspondence and decided not to respond. Or that he would write again in a day or two and tell her she was being silly and had no need to worry.

But being without him, even for a short time, had become unthinkable. Even more incomprehensible was the idea that she should marry and leave him behind. Her plan was to remain a widow until he came forward to claim her, or until death, whichever came first.

She could not tell him so. It was too forward, especially while she depended on him for her livelihood. He would think she was using him for the security he provided. But would it be any worse to use some other poor man, letting him take her to wife, while her heart had no room for anyone but Abbott?

She hurriedly signed, folded and sealed her latest letter, praying that it would move him to contact her. Was he really gone from her life without even saying goodbye?

Or was he simply waiting for her to come out and say the words of love that were always just beneath the text? How would she get him to make himself known to her, in person and not just in pen and ink?

There had to be a reason that he did not want to come forward and, as with the current absence, her thoughts raced trying to understand it.

Perhaps he was war-damaged, and unable to stand and fight for her. Of course, it spoiled her earlier belief that he had been at the ball with her. She could not remember seeing a crutch or a sling on any of the men who had attended that, and Edward had mentioned nothing of the kind. But there were disabilities to the body, mind and spirit that were not easily visible. He might be afflicted with one of those.

Or perhaps he was older than Edward had thought. An old uncle, just as he had pretended to be at first.

It made the most sense, but she could not bring herself to believe it. She had invested far too much of her heart and mind in believing that he was young and robust. Perhaps not handsome. But that would not matter to one who loved him as much as she did.

Or suppose that he had hidden himself among the three men he had chosen as her suitors? There was something so resigned in the paragraph of his last letter that she doubted it. It had sounded as though he was giving her away. And she could not remember meeting any of these three at the Fallon ball that she was sure Abbott had attended.

But if there was the faintest chance that he was offering himself as a possibility, she must be open to it. The idea was rather like a fairy tale, where the heroine had to pass a test to prove herself worthy of a prince. If she could not recognise him when he was standing right before her, then perhaps she was not deserving of his love.

She would go to the Melton ball as he wished her to and meet the men he recommended. If he was one of them, she would discover which and make him drop his disguise and admit the truth.

If he was not? Then he was sure to be somewhere on the guest list. She would be so charming, so beautiful and so witty that he would regret that he was giving her away and reveal himself.

Alex sipped his brandy and stared out over the crowd at the Melton ball, disgusted with himself and everyone else there. Since his last letter to Selina, he had been drinking far too much, and tonight was no exception. He had smuggled the spirit out of the card room and brought it out into the ballroom, where polite people were drinking champagne or lemonade.

But he had needed something to fortify himself if he was to watch Selina dancing and chatting with the men he had selected for her. Once she had made her choice and set a date, things would be easier. He would not have to see her at all if he did not want to. And he certainly would not write to her.

Except, perhaps, once. Just to congratulate her and to know that she was well.

No. Not even that. One letter would lead to dozens, just as it had before. If he wanted what was best for her, he had to give her up. Her recent letters had proven the fact, if nothing else had. She was as dependent on their correspondence as he was. The end of the last one had been blurred by tear stains, at the thought that he might be beyond her reach forever.

He had grabbed for his pen and scribbled two pages of assurances before catching himself and throwing the papers into the fire. Since nothing could ever come of their relationship, it was not healthy for it to continue. And if he set her free before she discovered the true identity of Abbott, he might at least know that she continued to love the part of him that had been her friend. That would be far better than letting things go until secrets were uncovered that would make her hate every fibre of his being.

There would be no more letters. But tonight, he could at least watch her from a distance and assure himself that she was well and having a pleasant time with other, more worthy men.

He took another sip of the brandy and stared across the ballroom at her, trying to be pleased at the way the evening was going. She looked happy, which was what he'd wanted, after all. And more beautiful than he had ever seen her. She was wearing an ice-blue dress, trimmed with silver embroidery that glittered when she moved as if she was floating on a field of stars.

At the moment, she was dancing with one of the men he had suggested to her, smiling radiantly at him, hanging on his every word.

Lord Stanhope had seemed like a good choice when he'd written the name down, neither too young nor too old, and with a decent income. Also, a squint, which Alex had forgotten when he'd suggested the man.

But Selina did not appear to be bothered by it. She stared up at him, her face alight, laughing at some inane comment he had made as if he was the wittiest man in the room.

Alex stared out at the dancers, forcing himself to look at other couples instead of focusing on each move she made, each time she stepped close to Stanhope, each time they exchanged a touch or a word. This was what he'd wanted. The plan was working. Why was it so vexing?

He felt a nudge on his arm and looked beside him to see his brother staring at him with an exasperated grin. 'Are you with us this evening? Or somewhere else entirely?'

'What do you mean?' Alex said, looking back at the dancers. The music was ending, and Stanhope was walking Selina back to a chair near the door.

'I have been speaking to you for a good minute and you have not heard a word.'

'Sorry,' Alex replied, losing sight of the couple and forcing himself to look at Evan. 'What were you saying?'

'Nothing important. Just that the evening is delightful, the company good. And you are scowling at the dance floor as if every person on it has given you offence.'

It was then that Alex noticed the pain in his jaw, probably caused by his clenched teeth. He took a sip of brandy and forced himself to relax.

'And how much of that have you had?' Evan said, staring at the glass in his hand.

'Obviously not enough,' Alex said, taking another deliberate drink.

Evan held out his hands in surrender. 'Do as you will. But it is not improving your mood, if that is your object.'

Alex sighed and handed the glass to a passing footman. A glance at the dance floor proved that Selina was standing up with another of his candidates, the unobjectionable Mr Henderson, who had more money than Stanhope and two good eyes. He turned back to his brother, forcing himself to ignore them. 'I apologise, my mind is elsewhere tonight.'

'Really?' Evan said with a knowing smile. 'Because

it appears to be out there.' He pointed to the crowd of dancers. 'Who is she?'

'She?' Alex frowned.

'Normally it takes a woman to bring out such a dark mood in a man.'

'There is nothing wrong with my mood,' he insisted.

'Like Byron on a bad day,' his brother chuckled. 'I have never seen you like this.'

'It amuses you?'

'To no end.' Evan patted him on the shoulder. 'Take heart. Whoever she is, she is bound to succumb to your charms in time. If you do not frighten her away with your sour looks first.'

In the distance, he was sure he heard Selina laughing at something Henderson had said. When he caught sight of her again, her smile was even more brilliant than before. 'There is no woman,' Alex said emphatically.

'Of course not,' Evan said, obviously pleased with himself.

'And even if there were…' Their eyes met.

She had caught him staring at her and she did not look away. His breath stopped in his lungs, his thoughts froze, even his heart did not beat, as everything about him tried to hold the moment for as long as he could. Then it was over and he turned back to look at his brother, struggling to complete the sentence he had started.

'You would not be in such a state over her?' Evan suggested.

'Exactly,' Alex replied, trying to see through the crowd that now separated them.

'Liar,' Evan replied. 'Fortune favours the bold and five years at Oxford have done you no favours.'

'What do you mean by that?'

'That you are out of practice in wooing ladies. Go dance with her, whoever she is, or someone else surely shall.' Then he walked away, leaving Alex alone.

She had been wrong.

If the first two gentlemen were any indication, this was not a test to help unmask Abbott. Mr Henderson and Lord Stanhope were pleasant enough, but there was no feeling of familiarity when she met with them. They did not laugh at what should have been shared jokes and hints at previous conversations. They merely looked puzzled.

They were impressed by her, of course. She had flattered and flirted, and did everything in her power to charm them. If Abbott was here, watching her, she hoped he was well and truly jealous.

And well he might be. Perhaps it was her imagination, but she thought she was being watched. As she spoke with Mr Henderson after their dance, she could feel a tickling at the back of her neck, like the breath before a kiss. Surreptitiously, she scanned the room, searching for the man who did not look away when she caught his eye.

The guest list of tonight's gathering was similar to that for the Fallon ball, and she was not surprised to see many of the same faces here. But though she danced with many of the same men both nights, none of them sparked the sense of recognition she had expected to find when she met Abbott.

Where was he?

At least she did not see Baxter when she searched the crowd. Whatever she might do tonight, she would not have to spend the evening dodging his attentions. But there was still the Duke of Glenmoor, whom she could not seem to escape. It was hardly a surprise to see him here. He was an eligible peer and could not avoid the attentions of the matchmakers.

Without meaning to, her eyes lingered on him, taking in his dark good looks. At well over six feet, he was much taller than her husband had been, with long legs and arms and a musculature that hinted at continual activity. It was strange because she'd heard that, before ascending to the title, he had been teaching at Oxford. She associated men of learning with a scholarly stoop, but he stood straight and wore his extra height with a relaxed confidence.

His hair was dark brown, almost black, and thick, worn short and tidy as if he could not be bothered with too much brushing. And his eyes…

They were looking directly at her now. She felt an embarrassing shock of connection.

She looked away, doing her best to pretend that she had not just been staring. It was not as if she wanted his attention, after all. She loathed the man, yet there was a certain something about him that drew her.

Sensing that she had lost interest, Mr Henderson found an excuse to depart, leaving her alone to wait for her next partner. She wished she felt something other than relief at his going. She could not marry the fellow, no matter how suitable Abbott might think him.

She spared a quick glance in Glenmoor's direction, then looked away again. He was coming towards her. It was as if she had accidentally summoned a demon or had pulled the cork from a djinn's bottle. What was she to do? It would cause a scandal if she ran from him, inciting even more comment than her snub at the last ball. She must steady her nerves and stand her ground and hope that he would go away again.

'Mrs Ogilvie.'

His voice matched his eyes, deep and rich. She would probably not be thinking such things if she had not had too much punch. In their last meetings, he had seemed polite but distant. But tonight, there was something in this ordinary greeting that spoke volumes.

She nodded in response, glancing up at him and then looking down at the floor again, suddenly unsure.

'You look lovely this evening.'

She could feel herself colouring at the compliment, which was even more confusing. She did not want to be flattered by this man, so why was she responding to his words? Suppose Abbott had been right and the Duke was in some way enamoured of her? He would think she was encouraging him with lingering glances and blushes.

'May I have the next dance?'

'No,' she snapped, trying to regain control of herself and the conversation. She held out her dance card to show him. 'I am spoken for.'

But the Duke was not interested in her carefully made plans. As usual, he meant to be in the way. He responded to her refusal with a non-committal 'hmm'. Then he reached for the little pencil attached to the card and struck through the name of the gentleman and wrote in his own above it. 'Problem solved. I claim the waltz, which is next.'

She stared down at the card in shock. The line he had crossed out, Mr Anthony Belleville, was the last of the men that Abbott had wanted her to meet. She should be outraged that he had spoiled her chance to question the fellow, but all she could feel was relief.

It served Abbott right. If he had been here, where she needed him, he could have protected her from Glenmoor and danced with her himself. She would write and tell him so when she got home.

But he probably would not answer.

And now her next partner had arrived and she was trapped between Belleville and the Duke like Charybdis and Scylla.

Before she could speak, Glenmoor chose for her, giving Mr Belleville a stern look. 'Apologies, sir, but I need a moment of the lady's time. You will have other opportunities to dance with her, I am sure.' Then, before she could object again, he took her arm and led her out on to the floor.

As he took her into his arms, she was surprised at his gentleness. When she had read of the reason for her husband's death, she had imagined Glenmoor as a brute. But as she looked back on their interactions, he had given her no reason to. He had been a perfect gentleman each time, offering aid and strength and asking nothing in return.

Tonight was no exception. His lead was commanding, but his hands were gentle, holding her as if she were as delicate as a butterfly and might be crushed by a moment's carelessness.

She had been strong enough, a few moments ago when she had been dancing with Mr Henderson. But with Glenmoor she felt shy and as fragile as glass. A sudden move, or an unexpected word, and she might crack. And who knew what might rush out of her if that accident happened.

Probably an embarrassing truth. What if she admitted that she had not wanted to dance with Belleville at all? That she was sure that none of these men was the one she was waiting for, that she was alone in the world and even more frightened of that than she was of him.

She closed her mouth tight against that possibility and forced herself to follow his steps. But not to smile, for that was quite beyond her.

He smiled back at her straight-lipped grimace as if she was the most charming woman in the room.

'There,' he said softly, so that only she could hear. 'It is not so bad to waltz, is it? I assume you have danced this before, for you are very graceful, even under difficult circumstances.'

She said nothing in response to this for, in truth,

it was still a shocking new experience to be so close to a stranger. Her husband had had little interest in dancing and even less in dancing with her. And she was not about to admit to that. 'Thank you,' she said, through gritted teeth.

'She speaks,' he said with a chuckle, and she felt a slight squeeze of her hand. 'You're most welcome. And it would be remiss of me if I do not tell you that you are the loveliest woman here.'

'You needn't bother with flattery,' she said, finding her voice again.

'On the contrary, this is just the time for it,' he replied. 'I often say such to the ladies I waltz with.'

'All the more reason not to bother.' It was nothing but an empty comment and without meaning. Strangely, this was disappointing.

'If you prefer, I will comment that the music is most fine this evening. And then you may tell me that you have heard better, if only to be contrary.'

'If you wish to hold down both sides of the conversation, it is not necessary for me to say anything at all.'

At this, he laughed again. 'Too true. It is tempting to do so since it is difficult to get a word out of you.'

'Because I do not wish to argue,' she said, glancing around her, still half afraid that this interaction would be reported in tomorrow's paper.

'Then I will give you no reason to. I am quite willing to agree with whatever outlandish stance you wish to take, if only to keep the peace. And as for my past with your husband…'

'I do not wish to speak of it,' she said, trying to pull away.

He spun them deftly, turning her moment of resistance into an elegant twirl. Then she was back in his arms again, held more tightly, so she could not escape.

'Well, I do. And now is as good a time as any, since you cannot run from me without causing another scene. While I have you here...'

'Captive,' she said with a frown.

'If you say so. But only for a minute or two. And before I lose you, I wish to apologise for what happened. It was not my intention to cause pain to a man who was already wounded, or to drive him to the action he took.'

When she did not respond, he continued.

'When we played, he gave no sign that it was anything more than an innocent game.'

'But it was,' she said, unwilling to give him credit.

'I am aware of that. And I know that it is not enough to apologise, and I do not expect absolution. But the words need to be said. I never meant him harm and would not have gambled that night had I known what the result would be.'

They made another turn of the floor in silence and she stared out over the sea of faces around them, wishing for anyone to rescue her.

No. She wished for one in particular, though she doubted that he would interrupt, even if he was here.

'It will be over soon,' the Duke said with a sigh. 'Too soon, perhaps. I suspect this will be our only dance and I cannot help but wish that it would last a little longer.'

'There is no point in wishing for anything,' she said firmly. 'In my experience, wishes do not come true.'

'How very sad,' he said with surprising feeling. 'Then, if I wish for anything, it will be that your opinion on that matter will change. After all that has happened to you, you deserve to have at least one dream come true.'

'That is an exceptionally sentimental thing to say,' she said, surprised.

'You were expecting that I would be otherwise?' he asked with a smile.

'I was expecting...' the worst. She had expected him to be like Baxter. But he was so very different and, for a moment, she almost felt...

What? Was it sympathy for this man, who had accidentally changed her life? Or was it something else? She felt a strange sort of kinship arising out of this stolen dance and she did not want it. It was too confusing and far too complicated. 'Never mind,' she said, and looked resolutely past him, over his shoulder and into the crowd, trying to focus her mind on anything else.

Next to her, he sighed. Then the music ended and he released her, before taking her arm again to lead her back to her seat. Once there, he held her hand, bowing stiffly over it, and said, 'Thank you again for favouring me with a dance. Better days are ahead for you, Selina Ogilvie. And if there is anything I can do to help, you have but to ask. I want the best for you. I always have.'

And then, before she could think of a response, he was gone.

Chapter Nine

After dancing with Selina, Alex made his excuses to the hostess and called for his carriage, not wanting to spoil a perfect evening by staying too long. Once he was away, he settled back into his seat to relive each second of the last few minutes to fix them permanently in his mind.

It had been paradise.

If he was to have only one partner in his life, he would have chosen her. And if he could have chosen only one dance, it would have been a waltz.

When he had finally worked up the nerve to go to her, there had been no verbal stumbles. He had not muttered about the weather or forgotten what to say. He had swept aside her objections and scuttled the competition in a way that would probably horrify him tomorrow, but at least he had achieved his goal and had a normal conversation.

Better than that, she had heard his apology. She had not accepted it, of course. But with time, the seed might grow in her mind that he was not the villain

she assumed he was. Even in the short time they'd
danced, he had felt some small change. By the time
the music had stopped, she'd moved with ease, as
though some of the weight she'd borne at the beginning of the waltz had been lifted. After a few minutes
in his arms, she had almost seemed to be content.

He must find a way to ask about the Duke, in his
next letter.

Then he remembered that he had sworn not to
write to her. And did he really want to read her answer, if she sent one? The truth of her current feelings might be so far from his that it would spoil the
glow of this moment and the feeling that, if he continued these tentative attempts to win her, he might
ultimately succeed.

He smiled to himself and shook his head. If another
letter arrived, in a day, a week or a year, he would read
it immediately, just as he had all the others. It was
one thing to deny himself the pleasure of answering
her and quite another to deny her the help that he had
sworn to give her. Abbott would always be there for
her, whether she wanted the Duke or not.

It was nearly dawn when Selina arrived home from
the ball and she was exhausted and yet unable to
sleep. She had done what Abbott had asked of her
and spoken to the men on his list. Before the night
had ended, she had even managed a dance with the
one that Glenmoor had frightened away.

Unfortunately, that man had been as disappointing as the other two. All were well-spoken and hand-

some, yet when she talked to them, she felt nothing other than a slight megrim from straining to be polite. Perhaps if she wrote to Abbott about them, he would have something more to say.

But when she sat down to do so, she was lost for words. It had been so easy to converse with him before he had sent his cursed list of names.

What was she to say now? That she could not tell one from another? Then he might tell her that she should let the men vie for her hand and let the winner claim her, as if she was a prize to be won and not a feeling human being. If she claimed she did not like them, she would be called too particular, for were they not all likable men?

The brutal truth was that, while they were likable, she did not find them lovable. She would not wait eagerly for their homecoming, as she waited for the latest mail, now. She could imagine becoming the rigidly obedient wife she had been for John, the happiness or sadness of her days measured by her husband's moods and her nights spent dreaming about a man she could never have.

She was still sitting at her writing desk with a blank sheet before her when the morning post arrived. And, as she had for nearly every day of the last year, she rushed to the front hall to receive it, hoping for just one more letter. As she sorted through the stack, she found nothing from Abbott. But there was a strange letter written in a businesslike hand with no return address.

Her curiosity piqued, she carried it back to the writing desk and cracked the seal.

My dear Mrs Ogilvie,
If you are interested in protecting the identity
of your mysterious benefactor, meet me in Hyde
Park at ten o'clock at your usual bench.
A friend

She turned the paper over again, searching for any indication of its sender, or who this mysterious friend might be. But the paper was unmarked and the seal was plain.

And did she have a usual bench? There was the place she'd sat when Glenmoor had interrupted her. If he had written the letter, why would he not have signed it properly?

It did not matter. If there was a chance that she might learn Abbott's real name, she could not help but take it. She set the letter aside and rang for the maid to help her into a walking dress.

When she arrived at the park, she went straight to the bench where she had met Glenmoor, trying not to look as excited as she felt. Finally, she was about to learn the truth about the man she loved. She smiled and it felt like the first natural expression she had worn in a full day.

'Happy to see me. That is an excellent start to our relationship.'

Her smile faded as Mr Baxter dropped into the seat beside her and stared at her expectantly.

'I was waiting for someone,' she said, hoping he would take the hint and go away.

'A friend,' he confirmed. 'Someone who sent you a letter just this morning.'

'You,' she said, her hopes falling.

'Me,' he agreed, grinning back at her. 'You don't have the Duke to protect you today, I see,' he added. 'Nor have you brought that strapping footman to turn me away.'

She was regretting that very fact. But it was probably time that she learned to defend herself against this man, since she could not count on anyone else to help her. 'You will have to take my word that your attentions are not welcome,' she said, keeping her head high and defiant.

At this, he laughed, and showed no sign of budging from the spot next to her. 'Then it is about time that you learned to be less particular. You are a woman without means, after all, and dependent on whatever man is willing to give you charity.'

The description was too close to the truth for her sake. But how was she to respond to it? 'I have friends who are concerned for my welfare.'

'Is that what you call the man who assists you?' he said, giving her a sidelong look. 'And what do you do to maintain such a close friendship? There are rumours about that you have a line of credit at a bank and yet you have no family to leave you an inheritance, nor did your husband.' He gave her another revolting smile. 'Unless you have become a shopgirl in secret and are earning your own way, you must be doing something to reciprocate for the generosity of your benefactor.'

In his letter, he had claimed he knew about Abbott. And he spoke with the air of someone who had more details than she did. Was there a way to get information out of him, without giving any more of the truth away? 'You seem to think yourself well-informed as to the details of my life,' she said, choosing her words carefully.

'I make it my business to be,' he said smugly.

'And why is that?'

He rolled his eyes. 'Really, my dear Selina, you must be aware of how I feel about you. I was captivated by your beauty, even before your husband died.'

At the idea that he had been observing her before her widowhood, she could not help a shudder. 'I had never spoken to you. I did nothing to encourage such an interest.'

'And your late husband did nothing to protect you from it. He gambled your life away without a second thought.'

'I was not a part of his wagers, to be bartered to a stranger,' she said, glaring at him.

'You might as well have been. If he had cared what was to happen to you, he would have left you something to live on. And your current protector is doing very little to help you, other than placing that enormous footman at your door.'

'He is not my protector,' she blurted. 'I have not even met him.'

'If he truly cared about you, he'd have made some honourable offer, instead of leaving you open to rumours.'

Were there rumours? She had seen no sign of them last night at the ball, nor had she read anything in the papers. But perhaps people had begun to speculate, as Baxter had. She felt a flash of annoyance towards Abbott for putting her in this position, before remembering that, without him, she would likely be in the workhouse, or living off the charity of the church. Or, worst of all, accepting Baxter's first offer of protection.

There was nothing she could do at the moment other than to look blankly at him and say, 'You are hardly one to judge what best I am to do with my life. Nor do I wish any more letters from you, nor any more insidious hinting about my future.'

'Then you had best make a break from the man who is supporting you,' he said with a mocking shake of his head. 'Because I have uncovered the details of your little arrangement and the name of the man who is caring for you. If you continue to resist me, I will share them with all who will listen, and what is left of your reputation will be forfeit.'

He knew Abbott. Or at least he claimed to. For a moment, the thrill of that blocked out her fear of the revelation. If he told the world, she would learn the truth as well. Then she realised that he was bargaining to keep the secret rather than reveal it.

She took a breath to steel her nerves and said, 'I will never give in to you, no matter what you threaten.'

'Are you sure your friend would be so cavalier if his name is made public? If he leaves you over this…'

'He will not leave me,' she insisted. But was that true? She had not heard from him in over a week. It was possible that he'd left her already.

'Are you sure? If you are wrong, he will leave you with nothing. And then you might not be so particular about the next man in your bed.'

'He is not sharing my bed,' she blurted, then looked quickly around her to be sure that no one had heard.

'Am I to believe he helps you from the goodness of his heart?' Baxter laughed. 'He wants the same thing I do. If he has not yet collected his debt, then it is only a matter of time.'

None of his suppositions proved he knew anything more about Abbott than she did. There was only one way she would know for sure and that was if she let him reveal the truth he claimed to have. 'You don't know him as I do,' she said firmly. 'He will not leave me. And I will never accept you even if he does.'

Baxter's face darkened. 'If I cannot get affection, I will settle for revenge. Come to me willingly or I will see to it that no one else will want you. Not for anything proper at least.' Then he deliberately laid his hand on hers, offering a squeeze before withdrawing it and rising. 'I will give you until this evening to make your decision. If I do not hear from you, you will see your own name in the scandal sheets tomorrow.'

Then he turned and walked away.

She sat there alone for a moment, trying to hide her shivers, forcing a false smile on to her face lest passers-by wonder at her pallor. What was she to do?

She must write to Abbott, of course, to tell him that Baxter was aware of his help and meant to interfere in their arrangement. He must not be caught unawares by the revelation of his identity.

But would he write back? His answer the last time she had complained of Baxter was that she must marry. But even he must know that could not be done in a week. Would he find the motivation to intervene when his own name was in the paper alongside hers?

She rose and walked home slowly, greeting the very large footman whom Abbott had installed at her front door to prevent just the thing she had gone off to do on her own. She smiled up at the fellow and said, 'If a Mr Baxter comes, I am not home to him. Now or ever.'

The servant grinned and cracked his knuckles. 'Of course, Mrs Ogilvie.'

Then she went inside, went up to her room and did not come down until supper.

Chapter Ten

It had been two days since her meeting with Baxter and she had not slept well on either night. It was clear that he meant her harm and, if his threat was serious, there was nothing she could do to stop him from destroying her reputation.

Half a dozen times she had started and abandoned a letter to Abbott, explaining the danger they were in. It was possible that he was married, or perhaps a member of the clergy, and public association with her would be embarrassing to him as well.

But he was the one who had started this. He was the one who had abandoned her, of late. It served him right if he was shocked to find himself uncovered by Baxter and without a plan to fix things.

There was also a niggling, unworthy fear that if she told him what was about to occur, he would abandon her again, deny everything and throw her to the wolves. She had trusted him for so long that her heart did not want to believe it was possible. But there was a chance that he was a man as unworthy as Baxter and she was better off without him.

In any case, she would know the truth if and when Baxter carried out his threat and told the world that Selina Ogilvie was a kept woman.

She came down to breakfast, tired and wan, to find a single letter awaited her in the morning post. As usual, it bore no return address. She thought of the letter she had sent, begging for news from Abbott. What if her worst fears had come true? He was dead and some solicitor was writing to tell her of the fact.

Then she recognised the hand from Baxter's cryptic note earlier in the week.

She opened it and read.

Have you seen today's scandal column? There is an item that may interest you.
Bernard Baxter

For a moment, she could not do anything more than stare at the words, frozen in place. The moment had come. Then she came back to herself and rang for the maid to bring her a copy of *The Times*.

She laid it flat on the dining table and stood poised above it, gathering her courage. Then she turned to the society page, her hands trembling against the paper.

She was ruined. But at least she would finally know who Abbott was. And if he was the man she hoped he was, he would come to her and make this all right. Her three suitors had not been the fairy-tale test she'd hoped for, but this was. She was in danger, for all the world to see. And now was the time for her knight in shining armour, her handsome prince, her clever hero, to come to her rescue.

It has been discovered that a certain gentleman has been providing for the widow of the late Mr O. for almost a year now. Apparently, it was not enough that he forced her husband to suicide. Or perhaps that was the reason behind the act. For Mrs S. O. is said to be quite beautiful...

Her name had been abbreviated to give the illusion of privacy, but it was no better than a fig leaf for that. Everyone would know who the on dit was referring to, even her friends. She read on.

...and since the Duke of G. is a notoriously devious man, we can guess what he wants from the poor widow.

She stared down at the newspaper in disbelief. It was nonsense of course. Baxter had it wrong. Of all the people she had imagined, it could not be him.

She was halfway to her writing desk before the wording of the item penetrated her consciousness. There was no point in writing to Abbott ever again. Her lover had been an illusion and her love for him a sick joke.

If she had been supported by the Duke all this time, then the letters had come from him as well. He had not just ruined her reputation; he had tricked her into revealing her innermost thoughts. He'd let her pour out the contents of her heart to him, sometimes two and three times a day for months.

And her most recent letters had been the most revealing of all. She had begged him for another letter, prostrated herself over his departure from her life. She had wept for him.

Thinking about it, she felt naked, vulnerable. She had not wanted anything to do with the man, but he had found a way into her life and upended it. She had thought that he could not do anything worse to her than he had already done, and now? This.

She owed him. Money and more. She did not have a penny to repay him, nor would there be a marriage to release her from his grip. No one would want her.

'The Duke of Glenmoor is here for you, madam.' The housekeeper made the introduction in an awed whisper, happy to be announcing a member of the peerage, even one as reprehensible as this.

If someone saw him coming or going from the house, the gossip would only increase. She raised a limp hand to her forehead and closed her eyes. Then she said, in the strongest voice she could manage, 'Tell him to go to perdition.'

'I am afraid it is too late for that, Mrs Ogilvie.' He was standing in the doorway of her tiny dining room, blocking the way to the stairs. She could not escape him. And, damn him, his voice was as deep and velvety as it had been at the ball. It showed no sign of the panic she was feeling at the most recent turn of events. 'You need me here.'

'Your Grace,' she snapped, pulling her hand down from her face, straightening her spine and wheeling on him. 'Or should I call you Mr Abbott.'

There was an awkward pause where his mouth worked, but nothing came out. Then he smiled weakly back at her and shrugged.

'Tell me it is not true,' she demanded, staring at him for what seemed like the first time.

'I cannot,' he said, holding his hands out helplessly before him. 'When I first saw you, a year ago, you clearly needed help. But I knew you would not accept that help from me.'

'So you created a whole new identity to trick me into depending on you,' she said, disgusted with him and with herself for being foolish enough to fall for the ruse.

'To help you,' he repeated. 'It was not a trick. It was…' He shook his head as if he could not tell her what his motivation had been. 'I meant no harm.'

'Given your history with my family, do not dare claim to be unaware of the damage you cause,' she snapped. 'That is just an excuse you use when you have done something unforgivable.'

His eyes darkened for a moment, as if he stifled some sharp retort. But when he spoke, his voice was as mild as it ever was. 'I did not mean your husband harm and I certainly have nothing against you. I tried to tell you, you know. Each time I saw you. When I could not find the words to say it, I hoped you would guess on your own.'

'More the fool you,' she said.

'I know I have made a muddle of things and I mean to make them right.'

'I don't know how you can,' she said, frustrated. 'You have rendered me utterly dependent on your aid. The world now views me as your whore. No man will offer anything but that.'

'But what if you could marry?' he pressed. 'Would you do it?'

'To one of your insipid friends?' she said with a scoff. 'Of course I would. It is that or accept Baxter the next time he comes sniffing at my door.' Or she could simply become what the world already thought she was: Glenmoor's mistress.

She shuddered at the dark surge of emotion that accompanied that thought. Would it really be so horrible to give up and become a creature of pleasure? She could imagine herself naked, fists balled in the satin sheets as she awaited her true fall from grace, fingers opening in shock at the wave after wave of satisfaction that would follow it.

She blinked the fantasy away and stared at the Duke, who was having no such dreams. His eyes were dark and his mood unreadable. 'Baxter,' he said in a cold, hard voice. 'He will pay for what he has done.'

'Do you mean to call him out?' she said, worried. 'That would render me infamous, if I am not already. It will make things even worse than they are.'

'I will find another way to hurt him,' he said. 'A way that does not punish you as well. But he will pay. You can be sure of it.'

She sighed in frustration. Why did it always seem that men could not see further than their own pride when things were darkest? 'How wonderful for you. For both of you, in fact. Go enjoy your vengeance and leave me alone.' She pointed towards the door, hoping he would take the hint and leave.

'But that is not all,' he insisted, and his mood changed again. He was shifting from foot to foot like an embarrassed child.

'Then please, finish what you have to say.' *And leave.* She left the last unspoken, indicating it with a roll of her eyes and a wave of her hand.

'I mean to put you beyond Baxter's reach,' he said with a nervous smile. 'Mrs Ogilvie…' He paused and wet his lips. 'Selina. If you would marry, then marry me.'

She could not help it. She laughed. 'You can't be serious.'

'I am,' he assured her.

'You are the man who ruined my husband,' she said. 'I cannot… I would not… The two of us?' She shook her head. 'I would never.' But hadn't she just imagined something even worse?

'I understand the damage I have done to you and your family. I know I have done nothing to deserve your affection, or even your respect.' His words were coming faster now, as he warmed to the topic. 'But if we were to marry, you would be permanently safe from Baxter and any other man who might think to abuse you.'

'I would be married to you,' she reminded him.

And he would own her until she died, body and soul, in a way that he would not, should she simply become his mistress.

'You would be a duchess,' he said in a coaxing tone.

'An honour I never sought,' she reminded him.

'But an honour, nonetheless. No one would dare think less of you. And your son…'

'Do not dare to mention him,' she said, shocked.

'I have to consider him and so do you,' he said. 'Edward would have advantages that you could never give him as a humble widow, or even the wife of a lesser man. No door would close for him. He will have the best education, his choice of careers. His choice of bride.'

'Because people seek a connection to you,' she said, trying not to sneer.

He nodded and stared down at the paper in front of her. 'Yes. Despite the villain the gossips have tried to make of me, the title is all most people care about. It is not fair, but it is the way of the world. The same will be true of you, when you become my wife.'

He spoke of it so casually that it made her even angrier to be forced to agree with him. He was miles above her socially. And at the gaming table, he had squashed her untitled husband like an ant, totally oblivious to what he had done.

Now he was giving her the devil's own offer. A chance to sacrifice herself to get what she could out of him. Without knowing it, she'd already taken his money. With marriage, she could use his social status to her advantage as well.

People would be horrified at her mercenary nature.
She would be in all of the gossip columns as a woman
willing to forsake her husband and marry his murderer.

'You are already linked with me in the newspapers,'
he reminded her, as if he could read her mind. 'They
are calling you my mistress. I can think of no better
way to change that than to marry you.'

He was right. She could not forget that her reputation was already forfeit. No man would want her
as wife now that it was assumed she had been with
Glenmoor. Baxter was still expecting her to weaken
and take him in.

There had to be another way. She had but to think
of it. But she could not do that with him standing in
the doorway, staring at her with those dark eyes, as
if he knew the contents of her mind when she did not
herself. 'I cannot think,' she said, shaking her head
at him and backing away so that the table was between them.

He took a half-step forward, then stopped. 'It is
very sudden,' he agreed, in that soft, soothing voice
that seemed to vibrate along her nerves like the pull
of a bow on violin strings. 'You do not need to tell
me now. I will wait as long as you need.'

She did not need time. She needed to be able to
say no. But the words would not come.

'I will go now,' he said, and set his calling card on
the table. 'Send for me when you have made your decision.'

'Perhaps I will write you a letter,' she said, and saw
him flinch. Then he turned and left her.

* * *

When Alex left her house, he glanced back only once, half expecting to find Selina in the window watching his departure. But the curtains to the dining room were shut and there was not so much as a hand resting on the edge of them.

He walked on, all the way to Hyde Park, where he paced the length of the Serpentine, trying to burn away the frisson of energy coursing in his blood at the enormity of what he had done.

He had proposed. Finally.

On one hand, it had been inevitable. Abbott had wanted to do it many times. It was what she had wanted to hear from him. She had hinted often enough that she hoped they were more than friends and he'd known it was true.

He had written the letters suggesting marriage and he had not sent a single one of them. He had one of the better ones in his pocket at the moment, to inspire him for the conversation he had known he must have. He should have simply read the thing to her. It was much more glib than the blunt delivery of facts that he had managed just now.

He had known that the very idea was a disaster. No matter what he'd tried to do to make matters better between them, the best he had managed was to reduce her outright loathing to a mundane, simmering hatred. Even that small achievement was gone now that the world knew he'd been supporting her.

The papers thought the worst—that this had been some kind of insidious plot that involved driving her husband to his death so he might take the widow as his own. The idea was positively biblical. He'd had a good mind to write a letter to *The Times*, informing them that he had never met the woman, or her husband until the night of his death.

He could not explain what had happened after that. Her beauty had dazzled him from the first moment. But she was so much more than that. He had seen it in her letters. That was the woman he had fallen in love with. The one who spoke freely to him, who had shown him her unguarded soul.

Now her spirit was slammed shut tight against him and he might never see that inner light again.

The thought stung. Though she had mocked him for it, he knew someone who deserved to pay for the breach between them. He left the park for an address on Jermyn Street, an upper flat that belonged to Baxter.

The valet announced that his master was out and directed Alex to a tiny sitting room, where he waited for almost an hour before Baxter returned home and greeted him with a smug smile.

'Your Grace. This is an unexpected pleasure.'

'For one of us, perhaps,' Alex said, staring back at the fellow until he looked away.

'I assume you are here about the item in the paper?'

'Which I know came from you,' Alex said. 'May I ask how you came to the conclusion that I was supporting Mrs Ogilvie?'

'It was nothing more than an educated guess at first,' he said, still grinning. 'You always seemed to be there when I wanted to talk to her. It was very convenient.'

'I see.'

'But then, I happened to be playing cards with a clerk at your bank.'

'And I suspect he bet more than he could afford,' Alex said with a disgusted shake of his head.

'It is not my fault that the men I play with are not more circumspect,' Baxter said with a shrug. 'But I was graciously willing to accept information in lieu of payment, and this banker was there when you set up the line of credit for Mrs Ogilvie.'

'I see,' Alex said again, thoroughly annoyed. 'And you used this information to ruin her.'

'I warned her that this would happen, two days ago,' he said with a shrug. 'It was within her power to stop the revelation at any time.'

'By yielding to you,' Alex said, repulsed. Or she could have come to him. Why had she not written to Abbott?

Baxter smiled. 'This is really none of your affair. It is between her and me.'

'There is nothing between her and you,' Alex snapped.

'Yet,' Baxter said with far too much confidence. 'You will tire of her eventually. I will be there when you do.'

'On the contrary. I mean to marry her,' he said, with more confidence than he felt that a wedding could come to pass.

At this, Baxter laughed. 'You have persuaded her of that, have you?'

'I will,' Alex said, firmly. 'Know that if you bother her, you will be harassing the future Duchess of Glenmoor.'

This, at last, seemed to affect Baxter. His eyes widened and he let out a small, frustrated puff of air. 'You would not...' he said, too confused to finish the sentence.

'Marry her? You think that because you attribute your motives to other men,' Alex said with a smile. 'It is a weakness men like you often have. You try to drag the rest of the world down to your level. Let me add something I think you will understand. Once I marry her, if you come anywhere near her, I will make your life hell. And do not think I am threatening something as tawdry as a duel.'

He thought for a moment and added, 'If the papers are to be believed, I am notoriously devious. I will focus that part of my nature on the best way to bring about your ruin.'

This, finally, seemed to have an effect. Baxter went white and mumbled, 'I mean no harm.'

'No further harm, you mean,' Alex said, voice dripping with irony. 'Now that you have a view of the future that awaits for troublemakers, I am sure we will have no more need to speak to each other. Stay out of my way, Baxter. And leave Selina Ogilvie alone.' Then he called for his hat and stick and left the man shocked into silence.

Chapter Eleven

Once the Duke had left, Selina declared to the servants that she was not at home to visitors and went back to her room, where she threw herself face down on to the bed and wept. Her tears began soft and fast like spring rain. Then they came faster, accompanied by a storm of heaving sobs. She buried her face in the pillows to hide her wailing, for she did not want Edward to hear her. He, of all people, must not see what a fool she was being over a broken heart.

She had not cried like this since her husband had died.

And even that was not true. She had cried over John, of course. It was normal to grieve. But many of the tears she'd shed had nothing to do with his death and everything to do with her fears for the future and the baffling road ahead. She'd cried for herself when he died.

His absence, if she was honest, had not plagued her much. He had been gone from her for a long time already. Death had just made their parting irrevocable.

But for Abbott, she felt as though she would cry her heart out of her body. He had been her friend. And John, poor John, had never been that. He had been her husband and her lover, but he had never seemed particularly interested in her as an individual. He had not asked after her day or her feelings as Abbott had. He had not laughed at her jokes or amused her in response. And he certainly had not cared enough to rescue her when she was in desperate straits. He had created the problem and then he had left her.

Then Abbott had appeared out of nowhere, to save her.

Now she knew why. It had just been Glenmoor, trying to make up for his part in the disaster. The rest had been lies and nonsense. He had made her believe that Abbott was real. In a way, he had been, for he had lived whole in her imagination.

Now he was dead. She could not conjure him up, as she had so many nights in the last year, when she had dreaded being alone. She could not imagine his arms around her without thinking of the Duke. He had been her one true love for almost a year, and now he was gone.

And her heart was gone with him. Now that the tears were slowing, she was an empty shell, as if her soul had poured out of her like salt water. Her future was just as barren, a winter landscape where there had just been spring.

There was a cautious knock on her door and a maid delivered the afternoon post, offering her an encouraging smile as if there might be something there that would bring her back to happiness.

No letter from Abbott, she thought bitterly. But there was a note from Mary, a reminder that they were to take a walk in Hyde Park the next day, as they had planned. The knowledge that her friend was willing to stand beside her in this difficult time was the only bright spot in Selina's day, the only proof that there was a reason to get up and keep going.

When she went to the appointed spot, Mary was there on the bench, ready to meet her. At the sight of Selina, she stood and reached out to take her hands, pulling her down to sit beside her. 'Oh, my dear. What are we to do with you?'

'You have read the newspaper?' Selina replied with a worried frown.

'My husband did not want me to come to you because of it,' her friend replied. 'I told him that it was nonsense. I know for a fact that you were not Glenmoor's mistress and that there was nothing to the rumour.' Then she gave Selina a long, silent look, waiting for her to confirm that as the truth.

'I am not,' she agreed, feeling foolish. 'He was sending me money. But I had no idea who it was really coming from. He called himself Abbott in his letters. And I thought, eventually…' She bit her lip, unable to explain what she had expected.

'You thought there would be an offer of some kind,' Mary finished her sentence. 'An honourable one, of course.'

'Of course,' Selina said hurriedly. She had wanted marriage. But when it was dark and she was alone in her bed, she had wanted other things entirely. She was embarrassed at the amount of time she had spent fantasising about nights of passion with the mysterious Abbott. If he would have come to her, she would have given him anything he wanted.

But he had never asked. And now the Duke was trying to take his place.

'And all the time, you did not know who he was,' Mary marvelled. 'He is your secret correspondent, is he not?'

'No. I mean, yes.' Selina took a breath. 'I mean, I would never have accepted the money had I known who it was from.'

Mary gave her a baffled look in response, which suited her contradictory feelings on the matter.

'And now he has offered to marry me, as if that will make everything all right again,' Selina concluded, with a disgusted frown.

Mary stared for a moment, still confused. 'The Duke?'

'Glenmoor,' Selina confirmed. 'He came to my home and proposed.'

There was yet another pause, then Mary's face split into an amazed grin. 'But that is too wonderful.'

'It is not,' Selina insisted, staring back at her friend.

'All this time, he has been writing to you and you have harboured a *tendre* for him,' Mary said, giving her a gentle shove.

'I have not,' Selina said. 'I do not like Glenmoor at all.'

'But you liked him when he was writing to you,' Mary said gently.

'Well, I do not like him now,' Selina said firmly. 'I was sharing my innermost thoughts with someone I thought I knew.'

'But you did not know him,' Mary said, even more confused. 'You told me yourself that he was anonymous. Now he has revealed himself.'

'And I do not know what to do,' she said with a sigh.

'That, at least, I can advise you on,' Mary said with a bright smile, patting her hand. 'He is young and rich, and he is offering to save you. You must accept this offer of marriage and clear your name. The Duke has taken care of you before and he will take care of you now.'

'But…' Selina shuddered. 'He was the one who was responsible for what happened to John. I cannot imagine myself lying with a man who would ruin another like that.' But that was just another lie. When she looked at the Duke, she felt strange, expectant and very, very guilty.

'You will learn to feel differently in time, I am sure.' Mary wrinkled her brow. 'The title will make up for any scandal involving your late husband. And if you do not like lying with him, it need not be forever. Once you give him a son, he might not bother with you any more. You could pursue someone who suits you better. Many couples take lovers of their choosing, after the succession is secure.'

It would be just like Glenmoor to cast her aside when he had what he wanted from her. Considering the elaborate ruse he had concocted to force her into marriage, there was nothing she did not think him capable of.

But that did not mean she should disrespect John's memory by choosing this man, out of all the men in London, to be her next husband. 'I won't,' she said at last. 'There is no way I can go through with this. Not with him.'

'Well, I could,' Mary said firmly. 'I am sure, once you have had time to consider the situation, you will come round to thinking sensibly about this.' Mary was patting her hand again, this time in encouragement. 'There are many marriages in the *ton* that are little more than business arrangements. Perhaps yours will be one of those. That is, if you wish. If it were me?' Mary giggled and raised her eyebrows suggestively. 'The Duke is quite handsome, really. And rather dangerous.'

'It is not exciting to have a dangerous husband, if that is what you think,' Selina said with a disapproving sniff. 'When I married John, I made sure that there was nothing objectionable in his character.'

'Well...' said Mary with a small shake of her head, as if to say, *And look how that turned out.*

'My marriage to him was not all bad,' Selina continued, though the statement sounded weak, even to her. 'And what will happen to Edward?' she added.

'Did the Duke speak of him?' Mary asked.

'He promised to take care of him,' she said.

'Then you must trust that he will do that. Some men are far less accommodating when it comes to children from previous marriages. If he is already thinking of what is best for Edward, that is a very good thing.'

Selina sighed. Perhaps she should do this for Edward. But what of her own future? There was more to being the wife of a duke, she was sure. More advantages than disadvantages. But she could not think any further ahead than the wedding night and the marriage bed.

When she did not respond, Mary nudged her and said, 'Do you even know what you would do without his help? If you refuse him, whom would you turn to?'

That was just the problem. She could not think of a single person that would care for her. She would not even have Abbott, who might as well have vanished now that she knew his true identity. It was quite possible that the Duke would cut her off without a penny, if she refused him.

But there would always be Baxter.

'I have no one,' she said with a shudder. 'And I doubt that I will get a better offer, now that the *ton* thinks I am the Duke's whore.' Which they would not have done, had he not decided to meddle in her life. But if he had not…

'The whole thing makes my head ache,' she said at last.

'Living in a great house and having dozens of servants and no worries about money will do much to clear your mind,' Mary said with a reassuring nod. 'Say yes to the Duke.'

'Who I hate,' she added.

'And who will be bound by God and law to keep you for the rest of your days. You will have ample time to make his life miserable, if that is what you choose.'

And he did deserve some misery, after what he had done to John and after the trick he had played on her by inventing Abbott. Normally, a duke was above the law and far out of reach of the censure of ordinary mortals. But as his wife, she would be inside this bubble of protection.

She would be able to pay him back.

For the first time in two days, she smiled.

Mary nodded back in relief. 'You are coming around to sanity at last. Do not brood on things you cannot control. For now, think of the ways that this can make your life better.'

And ways that would make his life worse. She would accept him, if only for that. He would live with a thorn in his side for the rest of his days and he would know that it was his own actions that had caused the pain.

'I will marry the Duke,' she agreed, with an emphatic nod. 'And I swear I will be the wife he deserves.' She smiled again, satisfied with her plan. Then she rose, reaching to help Mary to her feet. 'And now, let us walk and talk of other things.'

'Certainly, Your Grace,' Mary said with a giggle, and changed the subject.

* * *

A day passed. And then another. And still he heard nothing from Selina.

Alex's palms itched to write a letter, as he used to, before she'd known who he was. The habits of a year were hard to break, especially habits as pleasant as writing to Selina had been.

Now that he'd stopped, he felt like an opium addict who had given up the pipe. He was adrift and alone and with the growing fear that she would never contact him again. If she spurned him, what would he do? Would he have to watch her founder without his help, to see her reputation tarnished by what he had done to it?

He would not allow that. He did not know what he would do if she did not accept marriage, but he would never abandon her.

In any case, it was too late to go back to the happy time they'd had together when they'd exchanged letters. The part of his life where he had been Abbott was gone, just as his time as a don at Oxford had ended.

He'd been happy then, too, even though he had expected a future without wife and children, his life devoted solely to learning. There had been something very satisfying about having nothing but the higher calling of philosophy to guide him. He no longer had to measure his success against the impossible standards set by his stepfather, the old Duke of Fallon.

When that man had deigned to notice him, it had been to compare Alex to his own son and to find him wanting. Fortunately, Evan had had none of his father's prejudices and had embraced him as brother from the moment they'd met. He had been totally supportive of his plans to teach, other than a fit of laughter when Alex had entailed the requirements of the position.

'Celibacy?' Evan had said, doubling over with mirth. 'You?'

'I admit it will be a change,' he'd said, for in his early years he had never wanted for female companionship. 'But I will have my books for company. And friends, of course.' His life would be ruled by a search for wisdom and he'd been secure in the knowledge that it would never hurt him the way people could.

'How very satisfying,' Evan had responded, still laughing. 'You must tell me how it works out for you.'

It had worked well enough for five years. And then his cousin had left him the coronet and he'd been reminded that the rules for a peer were the very opposite of those for a don. The goal was to be fruitful and multiply. To create and procreate, and leave something behind when one died, other than scholarly writings.

And if she said yes, he would do that with Selina.

He sat down at his desk, surprised at how moved he was by the thought of being with her. It was more than he'd ever imagined, yet everything he wanted. In a few days, he might come to her as a worthy supplicant. He would break the long, romantic drought he'd been experiencing to hold her in his arms. He would be able to kiss that white throat and bury himself in her body.

He was awed. He was honoured. And he was most definitely aroused.

'Your Grace.' When he looked up, the butler stood politely at the door of his study, awaiting his acknowledgement.

Alex nodded, wiping the silly grin from his face.

'A Mrs Ogilvie wishes to speak to you.'

His passionate reaction withered as quickly as it had grown. His mouth went dry and his hands became clammy. He eyed the brandy bottle and rejected it. Whatever she had to say, he must accept it in cold sobriety. 'Show her to the red salon. I will be there directly.'

He waited five minutes, until he was physically and mentally in control again, then made his way to the room where his future awaited.

When he entered the salon, she was standing by the fireplace, her hand on the mantel as if she needed the marble shelf for support. Their eyes met in the mirror above the fireplace and he saw her look of worry replaced with resolve as she stared back at him.

He walked to a chair by the fire and gestured to the sofa.

She shook her head and walked to the centre of the room, but did not sit.

This did not bode well. But he nodded in agreement and shut the door behind him, standing with his hands behind his back. 'Have you reached a decision?'

She nodded, pausing for so long that his nerves were near the breaking point before she spoke.

'I will marry you.'

He breathed a sigh of relief.

'On one condition.'

Condition? He was the one saving her reputation. If anyone was to set a condition on the terms of their union, it should be him. But it was Selina he was marrying and there was nothing on earth he would not do if it meant being near her.

He took another breath and said, 'Go on.'

'It will be a marriage in name only. I will never love you. And I will never lie with you.'

She could not be serious. He waited, expecting her to admit that she was being unrealistic so that he might bargain anything else away but the thing she had just said. But she stayed silent, staring at him with those magnificent grey eyes. 'And what of all the things you wrote to me?' he said. 'Your feelings were quite different in your letters.'

'I made no promises,' she said, straight-faced. 'And the man that I wrote to made no offers.'

'Me,' he reminded her. 'You wrote to me.'

She shook her head. 'I would never have said those things if I had known it was you.'

He had known that was true. But to hear her say it still hurt. 'The man you expected to find did not exist.'

'I am painfully aware of the fact,' she said, staring at him in disgust. 'Because of your deception, I have no choice but to marry you. But I am not doing so willingly and I will not let you forget the fact.'

What had he expected? If he'd thought that she would dismiss all that had happened and forgive him, he had been a fool. He had only wanted to help. But she was right—he had left her no choice but marriage.

But could he accept the union she demanded? Even if he could live without the marital act, to forgo children went against all his title required and all he had wanted for himself. When he'd left Oxford, it had pleased him to know that at least he would have a family, a dream he had given up when he'd begun teaching. Now he must give up that dream again.

But he could do it. He would do anything she asked, if it meant that her reputation was restored and she remained safe from Baxter and men like him. It would be like being a don again. Then he had been a celibate follower of knowledge. Now he would be a monk, worshipping at the feet of an unfeeling goddess who longed to see him suffer. And he must never let her know. If he did, she might find a way to make his life even worse.

He schooled his face to show none of the turmoil he was feeling and said, 'As you wish.'

'You agree?' She seemed honestly surprised by the fact, as if she had come to him expecting to be refused.

'You have my word,' he said, staring back at her, daring her to look away.

'When must I…? Will we…?' She was flustered now. Apparently, she had made no plans as to what would happen if he accepted her offer.

'I will take care of everything. An announcement of our engagement will be posted in *The Times*, and a special licence will be procured. The wedding will be at St George's. The whole matter will be settled inside a week.'

'But all my things…'

'Will be brought here. I will explain the situation to my servants, and footmen will be dispatched to help you with the move. Positions will be found for your staff in my household. There is nothing to worry about.'

He waited for a moment to see what other excuses she might make. When there were none, he said, 'And now, if you will excuse me, I have other business to attend to.'

'Of course,' she said in a faint voice, as he escorted her to the door and out of his house.

When she was gone, he went back to his study and sank into the desk chair, stunned. He had agreed to the impossible. He was going to marry the most beautiful woman he'd ever known, the woman whom he had dreamed of since the first moment he saw her. And he was to remain apart from her, living as strangers.

There would be no family, no heir, no days full of children and laughter. For hadn't that been what he'd imagined as he'd written to her, that she might some-day care for his son as she did her own? Instead, she meant to deny him that, to give him a house as cold and empty as the one he'd grown up in.

He slammed his fist against the desk, so hard that

the inkwell jumped. Then he unclenched his fist and released the anger along with the tension. If this was what she thought she wanted, then he would do it. Because there was a chance, the slimmest of hopes, that once she knew him better, she might change her mind and love him. That would be worth risking a lifetime of misery.

Chapter Twelve

A week later, with his brother as witness, Alex stood by the altar of St George's Church, waiting for the woman who would change his life.

He stared at the door, trying to control the tapping of his foot as he waited for Selina to arrive. He was not impatient as much as he was nervous. He would not be surprised if she changed her mind. He could picture her writing to tell him so. It would be the height of irony for her to crush his hopes with a letter.

In another life, before she had learned his identity, they would have laughed about the idea that she might someday leave him. She would have assured him that there was nothing he could do that would ruin their friendship.

He would have known it was a lie. But he'd have chosen to believe it and smiled as he wrote back to her, calling her foolish, but dear. Now all that was lost to him, and he had not felt so alone in years. Not since his father had died and he'd had to face his mother's new husband, a man who hated his very existence and took pleasure in reminding him of that fact.

'It is the bride who is supposed to be nervous, not the bridegroom,' his stepbrother reminded him, with a smile.

'As I remember it, you were not worried that your bride would show up for the wedding.'

'I was secretly hoping that she would not,' Evan said, shaking his head. 'I have since learned how foolish I was. And how fortunate that she agreed to marry me.'

'I already know that I am fortunate,' Alex said, staring at the church door and wishing it would open.

'But your bride does not,' his brother reminded him.

'I am sure the idea of marriage will grow on her,' he said, hoping he was right.

'Most women would be satisfied to become a duchess,' Evan replied.

'Selina is not most women,' Alex said, and could not help but smile. 'She is not interested in being a duchess. At the very least, I know I am not getting a title hunter.'

'But are you getting a helpmeet?' Evan asked. 'It is not too late to call off this farce and find another way to deal with the gossip.'

'You know that is not true,' Alex said firmly. 'As long as she is unmarried, her reputation will be suspect. It is because of me that she is at risk from Baxter. I cannot allow that.'

'Very noble of you,' Evan said, in a tone that made

the word *noble* sound like *foolish*. Then he added, 'I do not wish you to be taken advantage of.'

'I am a grown man and older than you,' Alex said, scoffing. 'I know what I am doing.'

'And that is why you have got yourself into the papers over Ogilvie's widow,' he said with a shake of his head.

Then the door to the church opened and Selina entered, accompanied by her son.

Alex felt himself leaning forward, unable to disguise the yearning he felt at the sight of her. Then the move was cut short by an elbow in his ribs.

'I see the problem now,' Evan muttered. 'It is as I always expected—you have feelings for her that go far beyond honour.'

'And what if I do?' he said, staring at the woman approaching up the aisle towards him.

'That is both the best and the worst reason to marry,' his brother said. 'It all depends on the feelings of the woman involved.'

Now they both looked to Selina, and Evan sighed. 'And this does not bode well.'

His bride was wearing a grey dress and had not bothered with flowers.

'It could be worse,' Evan said. 'It could be black.'

'With the special licence, she had very little time to buy a gown,' Alex said. But she'd been out of mourning for some time and had other more cheerful dresses in her wardrobe. It was hard to see her current choice as anything other than a display of ambivalence.

'I am sure that will change, once you are married,'

Evan said with a barely perceptible roll of his eyes. 'If she discovers she can hurt you with shopping, she will spend every waking moment on Bond Street. If not that, she will look for another way to wound you. She will lead you a merry chase and your life will be misery.'

'Thank you for telling me this now,' Alex said, eyes fixed straight ahead. 'I would never have realised it on my own.'

'It is only to remind you that it is not too late to back out.'

That was a lie. It had been too late from the first moment he'd met her. He had always wanted it to end like this, with the two of them at an altar. But he had imagined the smile on his bride's face and not the dead-pan stare she was giving him now, as if she was walking to her own funeral.

She approached cautiously, pausing at a front pew to install her son, who sat, legs swinging, watching him with curiosity.

He gave the boy a nod and a smile, hoping that their brief meeting in the park a few weeks ago had instilled some small amount of good will. Edward smiled back and patted his pocket, to assure him he still had the compass.

Then Alex turned back to Selina and felt his smile slip in the face of her obvious disdain. She reached his side, her expression unchanging, then looked up at him with resignation, as though she had also decided that it was too late to stop what was about to happen, and announced, 'I am ready to begin.'

'I brought Fallon and his wife to serve as witnesses,' he said, stating the obvious.

'We are family to Alex, after all,' Evan said in a warm and welcoming tone. 'We will be your family as well, now. If you need anything, do not hesitate to speak up.'

'Or forever hold my peace,' Selina supplied, probably aware of what everyone was thinking.

Evan's wife stepped into the gap in the conversation and smiled as if she had not just heard Selina's ambivalence, holding out a bouquet to her. 'I did not know if you had time to find flowers. Alex says you live in a small house with no garden. But ours...' She shrugged.

For a moment, Selina softened, smiling back at the other woman. 'The Fallon roses are very well known. I visited the garden myself when I attended your ball.' She took the bouquet, which was a marvellous arrangement of pink and white blooms, held it to her face and inhaled deeply. Then she handed it back to the Duchess to keep during the ceremony. 'Thank you for your thoughtfulness.'

She turned to Alex again, her face hardening, and said, 'It is time to begin', negating the doubts and stepping towards the altar.

Evan gave his brother a sympathetic smile and Alex stepped forward to take his place at her side.

He had heard the ceremony often enough at the weddings of others, but had paid it little attention. Now, as he was reciting the vows in the empty church, there was a solemnity and importance to it that he had not expected. He wondered if Selina felt the same, or if she was merely repeating the lines as they were fed to her and waiting for the service to be over.

She had been through this once already, with John Ogilvie. And she'd said surprisingly little about that marriage, even after all the letters they'd exchanged. Had she loved him? he wondered. Or had that marriage been as empty as this one?

As she said her part, her expression never changed from that grim frown that she had worn when entering the building. During the bishop's sermon on procreation, she stared at him with such intensity that the man lost his place and looked to Alex in confusion.

Alex offered him an encouraging nod, as if he had not noticed his future wife's foul mood, smiling hard enough for both of them until the officiant continued.

A short time later, the rite was done, the licence was signed and he was declaring them man and wife and encouraging Alex to 'kiss the bride'.

He had never been so nervous in his life. The kiss might be the last one he gave her, if things remained as he'd promised they would. He did not want to waste the moment on a peck on the cheek. But a church was no place for intimacy and he did not want to embarrass her or himself by giving her the kiss he wanted. So he turned slowly, placed his hand on her shoulder and pressed his lips to hers.

As he did it, he could feel her flinch.

He paused for a moment, to mark the solemnity of the event, then pulled away and let his hand fall to his side. 'There,' he said softly.

She blinked at him, her frigid demeanour cracking for an instant, and he could see something like real surprise in her eyes and perhaps a touch of fear. Then it disappeared again and she was as cold as ever.

With the ceremony over, the Duke offered his arm and Selina took it, along with the bouquet of roses that the Duchess of Fallon had been holding for her. The flowers gave her something to focus on other than the touch of the man at her side. She was strangely conscious of it, after the intimacy of the kiss.

She had known he would kiss her. There was always a kiss at the end of a wedding ceremony. But the knowledge was purely academic. She had not expected to feel anything from it, sure that it would be brief and polite, more a symbol of something than the thing itself.

But there had been a moment, when his lips had touched hers, where everything had changed. She had felt a spark of life striking her dead soul like tinder.

And then it had been gone again.

She gripped the flowers tightly and resisted the urge to touch her lips, longing for a mirror to see if there was anything showing in her eyes or face that would tell the others of the difference inside her.

Had he felt it, too?

He looked the same. But then, she did not think that men felt as deeply as women did about small things.

He escorted her out of the church and led her to the same splendid carriage that she had ridden in when they had met after the Mathematical Society meeting, taking her elbow to help her into her seat. Before she could climb up, Edward scrambled up between them, taking a seat on the far side and leaning out the window to wave at the passers-by.

'Edward,' she whispered, ignoring the Duke's hand and hauling herself up in an unladylike lunge to get to her son. 'Where are your manners? You have ridden in a carriage before and needn't make such a scene.'

'Not in one so grand as this,' he insisted, bouncing on the seat and making the springs creak, then he looked back at the Duke. 'You did not tell me that you were marrying the man who gave me the compass.' He favoured her new husband with a wide grin of approval.

She tensed as she waited for the rebuke that was sure to come and the reminder to keep the child in line and out of sight. She should never have brought him to the church, but leaving him alone with the housekeeper as she did something that would change his life had not seemed the right thing to do either.

But instead of demanding obedience, the Duke smiled back. 'You have it with you?'

Edward nodded. 'Mother said I could not have it out during the service.'

'And I will tell you that you cannot have it out at the wedding breakfast,' the Duke agreed. 'But we are in neither of those places now and it might be interesting to know the direction to my house.'

At this prompting, her son pulled the compass out of his pocket and carefully aligned the needle with true north, watching it turn as they wound through the streets towards the Duke's townhouse, where a meal had been set out.

The Duke leaned back in his seat, content, and looked across the carriage to Selina. 'The ceremony went well, I think.'

'Weddings are all the same,' she said, trying to remember what it had been like to marry John. There had been a similar feeling of panic. But then, it had been because of all the things she had not known about married life. Now it was because of all the things she did know. Was this man serious when he had agreed that this would be a marriage in name only? Or did he mean to fall on her like a ravening wolf the first time they were alone together?

More importantly, why did the idea hold such fascination for her? When she closed her eyes, she could imagine those long-fingered hands gripping her skin and those deep brown eyes boring into hers, as he demanded her surrender.

She glanced across the carriage at him and then quickly looked away.

'I am glad you brought your son,' he added, smiling at Edward again. 'It is easier to understand life's changes when one feels one is a part of them and not just flotsam in the tide of others'.'

Edward looked at him, confused. 'What is flotsam?'

'The things that break off a ship during a wreck,' the Duke provided.

'So, weddings are like a shipwreck?' Edward said, wrinkling his nose.

'That remains to be seen,' Selina said, glaring at

the Duke. It did not help that he was speaking the truth in front of her son for she'd had trouble enough explaining to him how things had come so far, so fast.

'Not all of them,' the Duke said, still smiling. 'Some of them are more like rescues. It is easier for people to survive when they cling together rather than floating alone.'

'And even better if one of them has a compass,' Edward said, totally missing the point.

The Duke nodded, trying to stifle a laugh.

'What the Duke means,' Selina said with an exasperated sigh, 'is that we were poor and now we will not be. We will be living in a great house with him.'

Edward's smile faltered. 'What will happen to my things?'

'As we speak, they are being boxed up, and will meet you in your new home. It will all be just as it was,' Selina said, forcing a smile.

'But better,' the Duke added.

Edward stared at him, unconvinced.

'And first, there will be a breakfast. With cake,' the Duke added.

The idea of cake for breakfast seemed to cheer him and he went back to watching his compass.

She stared at the Duke, annoyed that he had found a way around the boy so easily.

He looked back at her, smiled and shrugged. 'Everyone likes cake.'

In his defence, the cake was very good, as was the rest of the food. If she had to be the head of a household, it would not be a hardship to be mistress here. It would be ideal if it weren't for the man who she had married.

He sat at her side, smiling and polite, making sure that her glass stayed full and she wanted for nothing. She ate in silence, turning away from him to be sure that Edward was happy, his plate heaped full of delicacies and his compass properly stowed away.

He was still smiling from the carriage ride and looked down the table at the Duke, his gaze one part curiosity and one part awe. She wanted to shout at him that he must beware. That the man he might grow to idolise was in truth a betrayer who had made him fatherless.

Then she bit her tongue and sipped her wine and said nothing. She was doing this for Edward, after all. The Duke's promise of a school and a future for her son was more than she could have got for him on her own. Even with the monetary help of Abbott, she could not have been sure that she could have opened the doors for him that would swing wide for a boy sponsored by the Duke of Glenmoor.

When the breakfast was over, Fallon and his wife rose to go and the Duchess paused to assure her again that if she needed a friend, she would find one ready. 'We are both most fond of Alex and eager for him to be happy,' she said, as if totally unaware of the reason for the marriage. 'We want you to share in that happiness as well.'

'Thank you,' Selina said.

'And I am sure, given his past, that he will be an excellent stepfather to your son,' the Duchess added.

'His past?' She struggled to remember what she had heard of the Duke that might have brought about such a comment.

'He was a stepson himself, once,' the Duchess said with a nod in his direction. 'It was not a happy time for him and I am sure he vows that life in his own household will be different. When you have children of your own, he will know what to do.'

'Children,' she said in a numb voice. The Duke was unlikely to tell even his closest friends of their arrangement. When they did not have a family, the world would think him sterile.

Then she reminded herself that whatever unhappiness or embarrassment befell him, he had earned it by his duplicity to her.

She turned to the Duchess with a forced smile and said, 'That is good to know.'

'We will leave you alone now,' the Duchess said with a smile and a blush. 'It is your wedding day, after all. I am sure you are eager for us to be gone.'

Selina resisted the urge to grab her hand and beg her to remain. What was she going to do in this great house, alone with Glenmoor?

He came to stand at her side now, smiling at Fallon and his wife, his expression unchanging until their carriage had pulled away from the kerb. Then he turned to Selina, his smile fading. 'If I might see you in my study for a few minutes?'

She followed him down the hall into the room.

He gestured her to a chair and closed the door behind him.

She took her seat and waited for the storm to break. His polite façade could not last forever. Then she would pay a reckoning for pushing him to anger with her stubbornness.

Instead, he took his seat as well and looked at her enquiringly. 'How much do you know of the duties that will be yours, now that you are Duchess of Glenmoor?'

Why could she think of nothing beyond the fact that she was supposed to provide his heir? That could not be what he was speaking of. They had already settled that matter, hadn't they? For the moment, all she could do was stare at him blankly and wait for him to speak again.

'You will be responsible for managing the servants and running the household,' he reminded her. 'I assume you are somewhat familiar with those jobs, but on a smaller scale.'

She nodded.

'There is this house and the manor where we will go in summer. There, you will have tenants to visit and I will wish you to see to the more personal side of their care…'

He rambled on about visiting the sick, tending to the still-room and other harmless duties that did not seem particularly daunting. The idea of playing Lady Bountiful was much more comforting than being the recipient of charity had been. Perhaps Mary had been right and this was to be a business arrangement and not a union at all.

'And while we are in London, you will be responsible for our social life,' he concluded.

'Our life?' she said, surprised.

He was looking at her with a matter-of-fact smile. 'Our life. We are united now, in ways that you have obviously not considered. When we receive invitations, they will come to both of us and acceptances will need to be written. A schedule must be kept and I wish to leave that to you.'

She blinked, thinking of her limited acquaintance with the women of the *ton* and wondering what they would say about her sudden rise in stature.

'Unless, that is, you intend on hiding in my home, afraid of what the papers might say next of you.' He was staring at her now, waiting for some proof that she understood. 'The gossip will not stop. But if you wish to avoid the more salacious speculation about our marriage, I recommend you accept these.' He pushed a pile of invitations across the desk towards her.

She stared at them for a moment, then scooped them into her lap. 'Very well.'

'And we must throw a ball by the end of the Season,' he added. 'People will assume that you want to show off your good fortune in bagging me.' His face had not changed as he'd spoken, but for some reason, she felt he was laughing at her, somewhere deep inside, in a place she could not see.

'A ball. I have no idea how…'

'You will have to learn,' he said. 'Ask Maddie.' At her baffled look, he clarified, 'The Duchess of Fallon. She will tell you everything I have forgotten, I am sure.'

Silence fell between them. When it was clear that he had nothing more to say, she rose, automatically resisting the urge to drop a curtsy to him in deference. Why did she feel so meek? He had not ordered her to do anything. All the same, she found herself falling easily into the role of obedient wife and servant, when she had meant to cross him at every turn.

How had he done it? Was it some ducal trickery? Or was it simply that the requests he'd made were all too reasonable to refuse?

He smiled at her, as if aware of her confusion, and said, 'It is the title, I think. And this damn desk and chair. It is hard not to be intimidating when sitting here and equally hard not to be cowed when sitting on the other side.'

'I am not frightened of you,' she said, frowning at him to prove it.

'That is good. Because there is nothing to be frightened of,' he assured her. 'Despite what you think of me, I am not an ogre. And our marriage need not be unhappy, unless you choose to make it so.'

'This union was forced upon me,' she reminded him. 'It was this, or ruin. I am little better than a prisoner in this new life. Do not expect me to be happy in captivity.'

'You made the cage as much as I did,' he said, and she saw the slightest of furrows in his brow, hinting at unexpressed anger. 'You made no effort to contact me when you knew Baxter had discovered the truth. I might have stopped him, had you written to tell me of his plans.'

It was true. She had been so eager to discover Abbott's identity that she had been willing to risk anything. She had gambled and lost, just as John had. And now that it was too late to do anything, he was throwing her mistake back in her face. 'I am well aware of my mistake,' she snapped, and turned to go. 'And now I am dismissed, Your Grace?'

Behind her he added, 'Dinner is at eight. After, on nights we do not leave the house, we will spend the evening in the sitting room, as a family. I expect Edward to join us. And I do not expect any friction between us to be witnessed by him. Is that amenable?'

The last was delivered in a tone unlike the other statements. There was a weight to it that turned it into an unavoidable command.

'We will see,' she said, without turning back to him. Then she left before he could issue any more edicts.

As the door closed with a firm click, Alex slumped in his chair, drained. He should have spoken to her in the dining room, or the morning room, anywhere but this damned study, which was the most pompous and uncomfortable room in the house. He had meant to be approachable and friendly, and to have a perfectly ordinary conversation about the expectations of their marriage and her place in it. Instead, he had been pedantic and dictatorial, not at all like her beloved Abbott, who had listened more than he'd talked.

Like it or not, they would have to work together to repair the damage he had done to her reputation by his heavy-handed generosity. He meant to ensure that she was not just accepted as a member of the *ton*, but placed at the pinnacle of the social hierarchy. She was a duchess now, after all, and he would be damned before he saw her slighted by her inferiors.

None of his plans spoke to what she wanted. It was the same mistake he had made by helping her. He had only compounded it by forcing her into marriage.

He closed his eyes and took a deep breath, trying to calm his nerves and focus his mind. The past could not be changed, but the future could. He would do better by her. He must. If he was ever to have the life he wanted with her, he must take the time to regain her trust.

Chapter Thirteen

After leaving the study, Selina threw herself into her duties, if only to distract from the long night to come. She toured the house with the housekeeper, spoke to the cook about supper, approved a week's worth of menus and went to the morning room to answer the invitations the Duke had given her.

Despite herself, she felt excited at the prospect of managing the house and was relieved to see that the servants were devoted to the Duke and eager to help her adjust to her new role. This life could be a good one, were it not for the husband she would have to share the house with.

Then she went to the nursery to visit with Edward and found her son was as enchanted by the prospect of a man in the house as she was appalled by it. He was having his dinner early in the rooms that would be his own private kingdom since there would be no brothers or sisters for him to share them with.

He left his plate to show her the toys that the Duke had assured him he was allowed to play with and the maps and globes and astrolabe that were in the school room, and added the promises of the Duke that they would be even more interesting than the compass if he was inclined to use them.

'He has been here?' Selina said, frowning back at the stairs and wondering what reason he had for coming to visit with her son.

'He says the astrolabe is for sailors,' Edward continued, his eyes wide. 'And I told him that I would like to be one of those.'

'You did,' she said, feeling a moment of panic at the thought. He was only eight now, but she had heard of boys no older than fourteen who left their mothers and went to sea.

'He said that if that was the case, I must study very hard. And he said that I would have a tutor and go to a fine school when I was a little older,' Edward said, showing no fear at the thought of abandoning his mama to see the world.

'When you are older,' she agreed, resisting the urge to pull him to her and to tell him that she would never let him go.

'He said that he would discuss it with you at dinner and that I could come down after and be with the family for a while in the sitting room, until it was time for bed.'

'Did he?' She could not keep the flat tone out of her voice at this. Her plan had been to ignore the Duke's demand for ceremonial togetherness and dine upstairs before an early bedtime.

'You do not want me to?' Edward said, his eyes

wide with worry. 'When we were at home, you always let me stay in the sitting room.'

'It is not that,' she said quickly, not wanting to hurt his feelings. 'It is just that I do not yet know how the Duke wishes his house to be ordered.'

'But he said…' her son interrupted, undercutting her argument.

She sighed. 'If he says you are to come down after your dinner, then you most certainly may.'

Edward smiled at her and then hurried back to his table so that he might be ready to come down when he was called.

Since she did not intend to leave her boy alone for the evening, she would have to go downstairs as Glenmoor wished. It was already too late to eat with Edward and she could not simultaneously shut herself up in her room and keep an eye on her son. So she went to her room to dress, thoroughly annoyed.

Her maid, Molly, was already aware of her feelings about the Duke. She'd made no effort to disguise them while she'd lived alone. But tonight, there was something in the girl's eye that hinted at disapproval of Selina's position.

Had she been talking with the rest of the staff? Were her quarters and pay better here than they had been when Selina had been both master and mistress to her? Or was she under the impression that Selina's opinions had changed as easily as walking through a door or signing a marriage licence?

Tonight, she dressed Selina with as much care as she had for her first ball, taking extra time with her hair and fussing over each ribbon of her dinner gown to make sure that the bows were perky and pressed, so she might make the best possible impression on her new husband.

For Selina's part, she did not care what that man thought of her. But it was easier to face him knowing that her appearance was unassailable. She descended the stairs to the ground floor slowly, as if she were making a grand entrance that required ceremony. But if she was honest, she was simply prolonging the inevitable. From the foyer, it was just a few feet down the hall to the dining room, where a footman hurried to open the door to admit her.

As she entered, the Duke looked up from the book he had been reading, hurriedly slipping it beneath the table to sit on the chair next to him.

'Excuse me,' he said with a wry smile. 'Reading at the table is a bad habit I've got into in the months since I came here. It is very rude, but it made the room seem less empty to me.'

She said nothing in response, but took the chair opposite the one where the book rested, glancing down the long table at all the empty seats and noting that her place had been deliberately set beside his and not at the far end, as she'd imagined.

'It will be less running about for the servants if we share the end of the table,' he said with another smile. 'And less cold food for us, I assume.' He stared at her, waiting for a response.

She unfolded her napkin and placed it in her lap, then stared back at him, silent.

'This is going to be a long evening if you leave all the talking to me,' he said, still smiling. 'I was a philosophy professor before I came into my title and my friends assure me, if I am allowed to ramble on the subject, I become quite tiresome.'

'Do as you will. It is your house, after all,' she said, staring down into her plate.

'And yours as well,' he reminded her. 'You are mistress here and not some sort of prisoner, no matter how you choose to imagine yourself.' His smile tightened somewhat, as if he was still hiding his annoyance from earlier in the day.

She could not help the flush of joy she felt at finally being able to hurt him, even a little. His most irritating feature was his unperturbability. 'It was never my intention to become so,' she reminded him. 'I was happy enough where I was.'

'In a house that I paid for,' he reminded her, his voice crackling with tension. 'If you are content to have me run your life, it is much more economical to do it here than at a distance.'

It was as if they had been fencing and she'd finally drawn blood. She felt a moment's triumph, tinged with a strange bitterness, and the desire to do it again. 'I never asked you to take over my finances,' she snapped back. 'I did not want or need your help.'

'Because you were doing so well on your own,' he replied with a sarcastic smile. 'Perhaps you have forgotten how it was when I came into your life. You were destined for the poorhouse.'

'Thank you for reminding me,' she said with equal

sarcasm. 'I also recall that you were one of those men who helped land me there, by taking my husband's money.'

'Aha!' he said. 'That again. I suppose I should be grateful that you at least admit that I was not the sole cause of his demise.'

'If it were not for you...' she began to say.

'Then your husband might have found some other reason to end his life,' the Duke said. 'A man who would gamble away his fortune as your husband did was clearly not happy with himself or his lot.'

'He had no cause to be unhappy,' she countered quickly. 'He had reason enough to stay alive.' Suddenly, it felt as though she was the one who had lost control of the conversation. He was probing old wounds that she'd hoped to hide from him.

'He had a wife and son,' the Duke agreed with her in a gentler tone. 'For most men, that is more than enough.'

But it had not been for John. It was one of the things that kept her up nights, wondering. Had he even thought of them in the last moments of his life? Apparently, when the time had come to write that note, he had not, for there was nothing in it for her. No advice. No words of love or comfort. He had been thinking of nothing but his debts and how to escape them.

The man beside her at the table was quiet now, as if he knew what she was thinking. Then he said, 'I should not have prodded you just now. If I have forced you to remember something you would prefer not to, I am sorry.'

She shook her head, surprised that the hurt was still as fresh as it had been on the day John died. The feeling that, somehow, she had not been enough.

'It was not you,' the Duke said, his voice even gentler than before. 'There was nothing you could have done that would have made a difference.'

'You can't know that,' she said, staring down into her plate.

'I did not know your husband, but I have known other doomed men,' he replied. 'If they think of others when making that final decision, they convince themselves that what they are doing is the best for all concerned.'

'But if…' She had been about to admit the truth before stopping herself. If she had loved John, perhaps it would have made a difference. He must have known. He must have realised how she felt and acted upon it.

And why she would tell such a dark truth to this man, of all men, was beyond her. She stiffened to hide her vulnerability and glared at him, angry at herself for being so weak. 'I did not ask you for consolation, any more than I sought your interference before.'

He straightened as well, chastised. 'As you wish.'

'And what right do you have to tell my son that he should go into the navy?' she added, remembering the conversation from before.

'I did not suggest it,' the Duke said blandly, picking up his spoon and tasting the turtle soup they had been served. 'But he was put in mind of it by the playthings in his nursery. There are instruments of navigation there and a fine model of a frigate with tiny lead sailors. When I was his age, I had thoughts that were the same.' He looked thoughtful for a moment. 'Nothing came of it.'

'It is not his nursery,' she snapped again. They were still strangers here, after all.

'Is it someone else's?' he asked, locking her gaze with his own. 'Have you decided to give me a child of our own who will supplant him?'

'Certainly not,' she said, unable to help the shudder that ran through her at the thought. She hoped it would appear to him that she was appalled by the idea. But strangely, his suggestion had been like a fingertip run over bare skin, leaving her tingling and expectant.

'If there are to be no other children, the nursery is Edward's,' the Duke said, in a tone that was surprisingly final. 'And if you wonder at my authority in speaking to him of the future, it came to me when we married. I am head over the household, over both you and him.'

'You cannot force us to obey you,' she said stubbornly, before remembering that there were men like Baxter who viewed such words as a challenge.

'Do you intend to rebel against anything I might wish, or only the things you do not agree with?' he said, giving her a searching look.

She did not intend to rebel at all. She simply wished to have some say in her life. Between John and this man, it felt as if that might never happen. And if marriage meant that she would lose Edward… 'I have no intention of allowing you to pack my son off to school or the navy, or whatever you intend for him, just because it inconveniences you to have him here.'

This elicited a sharp bark of laughter. 'And I suppose you intended that he would stay in your shadow forever? It is an indication that he needed some man in his life. If he wishes to make anything of himself, he will need schooling. Sending him off to Eton is hardly a black-hearted scheme to get him out of my sight. It is merely what happens to boys of his class. He will go away to school and, when term ends, he will be welcomed home to see his loving mother wherever she might be at the time.'

It was better than she could have hoped for Edward with no money or connections. And if the offer had come from anyone else, she would have been grateful. Instead, she said, 'You should have discussed it with me first.'

He gave her a sceptical look. 'So that you could refuse me? I suppose you mean to fire the tutor I am hiring, so that he might keep up with his studies while in London.'

A tutor was a thing she had meant to hire with the money from Abbott. But while she had been in mourning, it had seemed like an unnecessary stress to add to their already confusing lives. Now that they were to be settled here, there was no reason that he should not be properly educated and prepared for school. But she had not planned to turn the raising of her child over to this stranger. 'I wish to speak with the tutor, before you hire him.'

He shrugged and took another sip of his soup. 'I see no reason why not. But I assure you, I would not choose anyone who was not suitable.'

'He is *my* son,' she said firmly.

'And my responsibility,' the Duke countered. Then he went back to his soup.

The rest of the courses proceeded in silence, with her smouldering over her food and trying to ignore the presence of the man she loathed. It was a shame that he was there, for it was the only thing spoiling an otherwise excellent meal.

Alex busied himself with his food, trying not to wonder what his bride was thinking. Dark thoughts, he suspected, for though the roast was tender, she sawed at the meat as if it gave her pleasure to stab something.

Tonight's conversation was, if not better than previous attempts, at least longer. He wondered if all interactions between them would be battles for supremacy, as this one had been.

It rather reminded him of his mother and stepfather. They had argued constantly when they were together and it had set the whole house on edge. When they'd chosen to live apart, it had been almost as bad, for he and Evan had had to contend with one or the other of them, still bitter but with no one to shout at but their combined children.

This was not the way he meant to run his own household. If she must hate him, she should learn to do so civilly. And he must not rise to the bait when she was not. They must find a way to get along, if only for the sake of the child.

When dinner was finally over, he led the way to the sitting room. As they left the dining room, he could hear Edward at the head of the stairs, as fidgety as he had been in the coach after the wedding. Before he could be summoned, the boy came galloping down the stairs to join them.

Selina gave a warning 'shush' as he arrived, as if awed to quiet by the grandness of the hall. He had to admit that he had felt the same when he had moved here. The house had seemed as staid and elderly as the previous duke had been, unaccustomed to little boys and their ways.

But that was about to change, or so he hoped. It was to be a home now, for the three of them, and not just a showplace. He turned as the child approached and said, 'It is all right.' Then he gestured him on ahead to a door on the right-hand side of the corridor.

They entered before him and he paused in the doorway, waiting to see their response to the size of the room, the ornate decoration of it and the comfort of the furniture. It was an impressive sight, with blue wallpaper and thick rugs over the gleaming white marble of the floor.

Selina lifted her head in defiance and drifted into the room, as beautiful as a swan, claiming her place by the fire as if she had belonged here all along. She reached for the basket of needlework that had been brought from her old home, selecting an embroidery hoop and some coloured silk, then set to work.

She might be fine, but there was nothing in this space for a boy to entertain himself with. Edward saw that immediately and lost his nerve, bumping into the Duke in his effort to get out and go back to the nursery.

Alex nudged him forward again. 'Go on. There is nothing to be afraid of. It is only family here to-night, after all.'

Selina's eyes narrowed as if she wanted to argue that they were nothing of the kind. Perhaps they weren't. It was not as if a few magic words said at the altar had made them compatible.

But they would have to find their way somehow. From her letters, he knew that she longed for this sense of family and stability. It was only him that she objected to. At the moment, she was staring at her embroidery with a deliberate intensity, as if she could make him disappear simply by ignoring him.

He turned to Edward, whose loyalty had been bought with a compass and a carriage ride. The boy had gone to the game table by the fire and picked up one of the delicately carved chess pieces from the board, turning it over in his hand. A knight, Alex noted with a smile. It had been the little horses that had fascinated him, when he had first seen the game.

'Do you play?' he asked.

The boy shook his head hesitantly.

'Let me show you.' He pulled up a chair to the table

and gestured to the opposite side of the table for Edward, then showed him the movement of each piece, spotting him several pieces at the beginning of the game and offering gentle corrections to prevent any egregious, game-ending mistakes.

At what age had he learned to play chess? He had known it when his mother had remarried and been the one to teach Evan when they were twelve and ten, respectively. That meant that his own father had taught him, though he could not remember a time when he had not known the rules.

Apparently, John Ogilvie had been too focused on games of chance to teach his own son. The fact annoyed Alex, as did the slavish devotion that Selina showed to a man who had neglected and betrayed her. He did not have to look up from the board to feel her disapproval of him now. He could hear the uneven tempo of her breath and the soft stabbing of her needle as it struck the stretched linen she was working on.

Was she thinking of him? he wondered. Comparing him to Ogilvie? If so, why was he found wanting?

Edward went to bed after three games. He had lost all of them, but did not seem bothered by the fact, kissing his mother and smiling proudly at Alex, who promised him they would play again soon.

Of course, his absence left Alex alone with his wife again and she seemed ready to argue. He ignored her and stayed at the board, painstakingly setting up the pieces for various gambits, running through a game against himself to pass the time.

'Speak,' he said at last, when her silence became too oppressive to stand. 'I know you have something to say. The air is pregnant with it. You might as well get it out and save us both the suspense.' Then he looked up at her and waited.

'I do not want you to talk with my son,' she said, bristling like an angry hen.

'I am aware of that,' he replied, watching her.

'You are responsible for rendering him fatherless and have no right to his company.'

'Perhaps,' he allowed. 'But now that I have married you, I am responsible for raising him, for paying for his education, his food, his clothing and his entertainment. I have no intention of doing that in silence for the next ten years.'

'I would never have married you if it were not for the article in the newspaper, and I certainly did not do it to burden you with the care of the two of us.'

'Having a stepson is not a burden,' he snapped, surprising himself with the vehemence. 'At least it should not be.' Then he looked at her directly, his fingers deliberately knocking over the white king with the piece in his hand. 'I speak from experience.'

'In what way?' she said, watching him closely.

'I was that boy,' he said. 'Or one very like him.' Now his fingers closed around a pawn, squeezing until his hand ached. 'The unwanted stepson of a powerful man. Evan's father would not acknowledge me when we were in the same room together, much less care about my future. It was fortunate that there was money from my late father to cover my education, for I doubt old Fallon would have paid for it.'

'I did not know,' she said.

'I have lived the life you would choose for your son and know that he will not understand the disagreement between us. He will think that there is a deficiency in his own character that renders him somehow unlovable. Is that truly what you want for him?'

When she did not answer, he shook his head. 'Then I misjudged you, for I thought that, of all things, you wanted what was in the best interest of your son.'

'But not to be raised by his father's murderer,' she snapped, still resisting.

'If that is what you still think of me, then there is little to be done to mend the breach between us. But there is no such division between Edward and me, and I refuse to create one. Like it or not, his real father is no longer here and it is better that someone step up and take over his job. I mean to do so, whether you like it or not. And now, if you will excuse me, I am going to bed.' Then he set the chess piece aside and left her alone.

It was exhausting to be cross all the time. It was giving her a megrim.

As her maid prepared her for bed, Selina rubbed at her temples, trying to relax the tension that had settled there. She was tempted to announce to the girl that there was no point in laying out her best nightgown or adding ribbons to her braided hair. No one would be seeing it. Nothing was going to happen.

This was not the wedding night that she was imagining for her mistress.

But that would embarrass her more than it did the Duke. He seemed to have adjusted to their loveless marriage with little comment. It was Selina who could not seem to manage her emotions.

She still did not know what to think about the way Glenmoor was treating her son. All her instincts cried out that she must protect the boy from the man she had married. But what reason was there to save him from chess lessons and the promise of an Eton education?

She dismissed the maid and climbed into her bed, staring up at the hangings, waiting for sleep and thinking of her last wedding night, which had been even more difficult than this one. With John, she had been totally unprepared for what had been expected of her. He had looked at her as if she were a fool, then pushed her on to her back and spread her legs, and a few moments later there had been pain and, with it, understanding.

The act had grown easier with practice. But his treatment of her had never been what she had imagined when she'd fantasised as a girl. She had learned how best to seek and find pleasure in their times together, and, in the end, had found it quite pleasant.

But there was no guarantee that it would be the same with a different man, especially one as selfish as she had assumed the Duke was. And why was she even considering it, since he had given his word that he would not come to her? The thought of lying with him was terrifying, and something else as well. Something undefinable, part-dread and part-excitement. She had to admit, he was an attractive man.

But then the devil was reported to be so as well. And the Bible was quite clear that temptation was something to be resisted, not brooded upon.

She rolled over, trying to clear her mind of the possibilities and get some sleep. Whatever was to happen between them, it would not be tonight.

Then, in the distance beyond her bedroom door, she heard a thin, reedy voice calling, 'Mama?'

With the instincts of eight years of motherhood, she was out of bed and into her wrapper, heading towards the door before Edward could call again. The last thing they needed was for the boy to wake the Duke and anger him. She did not want this odd union of theirs to be any more stressful than it already was.

'Mama?'

She was out in the hall now and could see her son, his nightshirt a ghostly white as he stumbled down the hall towards her.

'Here,' she whispered, hurrying towards him with a finger to her lips, urging him to silence.

'I cannot sleep,' he said in a normal tone, ignoring her warning.

He must have been too loud, for beside them the door opened and the Duke stepped into the hall, staring at the pair of them in curiosity. 'What seems to be the matter?'

'Nothing,' Selina said hurriedly, laying a protective hand on her son's shoulder.

'I miss my old room,' Edward said, ignoring her again.

'I see,' the Duke replied.

'There is nothing wrong with the nursery,' she said, almost over the top of his comment. 'It is better than your old room.' Bigger, at least. Of course, that was probably part of the problem. The whole house was large and the two of them had been swallowed up in it.

'We had to move when Father died and I did not like it. And now we are moving again,' Edward said, tired and cranky and hearing none of her assurances.

'It must be most difficult for you,' the Duke said in a surprisingly reasonable voice. 'Let us go back to the nursery and see what can be done to make it better.' Then he turned down the hall and led them back to the open door.

Edward hesitated on the doorstep, staring in with dread.

The Duke walked into the room, clearly unfazed, and went to the window, pulling the curtains wide to let the moonlight into the room. 'Does this make it better, or worse?'

The boy took a hesitant step over the threshold. 'I can see better.'

'With a candle, you could see even more,' the Duke reasoned, and lit a taper off the embers of the fire, fixing it in a holder on the mantelpiece. 'There, not so bright that you cannot sleep, but bright enough so that the room does not seem so strange. Do you need your mother to sit with you for a while, or should I send for a maid?'

The boy gave him a speculative look, then raised his chin. 'I am fine, now.'

'That is good to know.'

'Are you sure…?' Selina said, drawing closer to him, only to see him draw away.

'The boy says he is fine,' the Duke said firmly, giving Edward a smile and a nod.

'I will be better now,' Edward assured her, giving her the same closed-mouth smile.

'Very well,' she said with an exasperated sigh. 'But if you need me again, you have but to call.'

The boy climbed back into bed and the Duke shut the door, wiping one hand against the other as if pleased that the matter was settled. Then he looked at Selina and said, 'Do not worry about him. He just needed a moment's reassurance.'

'From you,' she said doubtfully. 'And what do you know about children?' For someone who had never been a parent, he had done surprisingly well.

'He is a boy. As such, he will not want to show weakness in front of me.'

'It is not weakness to be afraid in a new place,' she said, narrowing her eyes.

'Of course not. But that does not mean that he was not embarrassed that I came to see what was wrong.'

'Then you should have stayed in your room,' she said. 'He is my son, after all.'

'Are you telling me what I can and cannot do?' he said with a smile.

'Of course not.' Her eyes fell and she found herself staring at his bare feet on the carpet and travelling slowly up the expanse of equally bare leg that was showing beneath the hem of his dressing gown.

'Because I meant what I said earlier about being a father to the boy.'

He was talking to her now, but she could not seem to concentrate on the words. Her mind and her eyes were still focused on the sight of his legs and the fact that he seemed to be wearing nothing beneath the robe. She continued her inspection of him, following up the length of his body to note the satin belt slung low on his hips, tied in the most casual of knots, and the few inches of fabric that lapped below it, lending decency and saving her from the ultimate embarrassment.

She should not be staring there. She should not be showing any curiosity at all. But then, he was her husband and this was her wedding night. If things had been different, curiosity about his naked body would be perfectly natural.

But that was not what she had wanted. He was not that sort of husband, nor was she that sort of wife. He certainly was not ogling her in the manner that she was looking at him and she must do him the same courtesy. She dragged her gaze from his legs, only to find that she was staring at the vee of bare chest displayed by the same half-open robe.

As she watched, his words stopped and he sighed, clearly frustrated by her lack of response. 'It is late. Let us return to our rooms and to bed. I think your Edward is settled for the night, but if you fear not, there is no reason that you cannot go back to check on him and undo the damage you think I have done.'

'No,' she whispered in a hoarse voice. 'He will be all right, I think.'

The Duke gave his head a little shake as if he was surprised that she had yielded so easily. 'Goodnight, then.' Then he turned and went into his room, shutting the door behind him.

She hurried to hers and did the same, only to find herself staring at the connecting door between their rooms. Was he really naked, just on the other side of the door?

The question shamed her. She hated Glenmoor. The fact that he was a virile man should not alter her feelings in any way. But there was something about her newly married state that had awakened unexpected feelings. A carnal interest that aroused something in the depths of her, an urge that pushed her towards that connecting door. She approached silently, dropping to her knees in front of it, pressing her palms against the wood panel and putting her eye to the keyhole to stare into his room.

He was standing by the fire, the robe discarded at the foot of the bed, and he was naked, as she had expected. His back was to her and he stretched his arms above his head, giving her a view of the sinews of his shoulders, muscular arms, a narrow waist and the taut curves of his hips, the thighs and calves flexing and relaxing as he turned to sit on the bed.

She stifled a gasp as she saw the rest of him, the sculpted muscles of his chest and abdomen and lower, the place where she should not be looking, but from which she could not seem to look away.

The muscles of her own body tightened at the sight of him and the memory of what a man like that could do for her, if she allowed him to. One of her hands dropped to her belly and pressed tightly against it, smoothing down to touch between her legs.

Then she closed her eyes and turned away. This was not just any man she was spying on. It was Glenmoor, who had tricked her into dependence and into marriage, just as he had tricked her husband out of his life.

She clambered to her feet and crept away from the door again, waiting until she was well clear of it to throw herself on the bed and turn her face and body from the keyhole.

But she could not force herself not to imagine him. When she closed her eyes, she could still see the magnificent figure on the other side of the door, as if the image was etched on her very soul. At last, she could stand it no longer and pleasured herself, stroking until a fire rose within her and burned away the uncontrollable urges. When she was spent, she pulled the covers high and fell into a fitful sleep.

Chapter Fourteen

Alex had never been the sort to hold romantic notions about marriage, since he had never intended to have one. He had given even less thought to his wedding night. He had decided, long before Oxford, that if he desired companionship in bed, there were any number of women willing to oblige. It was a pleasant pastime, but there was nothing particularly sacred about it and no need to obsess about any one occasion.

Of course, that was before he'd met Selina. In the last year, he had spent far too much time imagining what it would be like to be with her. The first time would be a profound event, the beginning of their life together.

He had never imagined that he would spend the night reading in bed, trying to distract himself from the delectable woman sleeping just a room away. When he had seen her in the hallway, tending to her son, she had been wearing a nightgown of lace, her long blonde hair bound in a thick, beribboned braid that hung down her back, swaying as she walked.

The ensemble had been beautiful, but rather fussy for his tastes. He'd wanted to undo the ties and loosen the braid, to see the beautiful woman underneath.

But last night had not been the right time. He had married a widow and he had known there would be a child to care for. But he had not expected she would be so protective of her son, when he'd made it clear that he meant the boy no harm. It was not as if he had beaten the boy, or locked him in his room, as his own stepfather had done to him. He had been gentleness itself.

But by her snapping in the hallway after, she would have preferred discipline to kindness. Apparently, she would not be satisfied with him until he became the villain she imagined him to be.

If that was so, she would be sorely disappointed. He had no intention of compromising his values by becoming a tyrant.

Though the night was nearly sleepless, the next day passed easily, because he had reason to avoid her. He was up early for a walk in the park and took luncheon at his club, before the afternoon session of Parliament.

Evan was waiting for him at White's, the table set for two and his glass of claret ready. He smiled as Alex approached, and set down the paper he was reading. 'You are in the gossip columns again, brother.'

Alex winced. 'That was what I tried to avoid by marrying.'

'It is the marriage itself that is the topic. This time,

you are the "fortunate Duke of G." and your story is proclaimed to be "romantic".'

He winced again and hoped Selina had not seen it, for he doubted that she shared the view of the writer.

'And is it?' Evan said, his smile fading to one of polite enquiry. 'Romantic, that is.'

'It is as I expected it to be,' Alex said, dodging the question.

'That bad,' Evan replied, shaking his head.

'Last night, I played chess with the boy,' Alex said, evading again.

'Have you explained to him about the succession?' Evan asked. 'And about your connection to his father?'

'He has just come into the household,' Alex said.

'He has to be told. If his mother has not...'

'I do not know what his mother has told him.' But whatever it was, he could guess that it was not good. 'I will talk to him in time.'

'And what do you mean to do about the fact that his mother hates you?'

Alex started in surprise. 'Is it so evident?'

'Clear enough to those of us who were at the wedding.'

He sighed. 'She has reason enough to do so.' Then he told Evan about Abbott and the letters they'd exchanged.

In response, he received the derisive laughter that he so richly deserved. When Evan had wiped away the tears of mirth and regained control of himself, he said, 'I swear, you were much smarter about some things before Oxford. Never lie to a woman and expect her to love you afterwards.'

'I never expected her to love me. At least, not at first. But things got out of hand.'

'They certainly did,' Evan said, smirking. 'But to your credit, you write very compelling letters.'

'Abbott does,' Alex said, sullenly.

'And you are Abbott,' his brother replied.

'Abbott is a fiction,' Alex said, shaking his head. 'As such, he has no flaws and makes no mistakes. Of course she fell in love with him. But I?'

'You are a mere mortal,' Evan stated.

'I have created my own worst enemy,' Alex said with a frown. 'And I do not know how to get rid of him. I cannot help but think that she compares me to the man she expected and has found me wanting.'

'This is a conundrum,' his brother agreed. 'How do you intend to make her settle for a man who is merely young, handsome, rich and titled?'

'I have no idea,' Alex said, and took a sip of his wine. 'For now, I mean to have lunch. After that, who knows what will happen?'

By the time the Duke returned home from Parliament, supper was finished and Selina and Edward had already gone to the sitting room. Edward was entertaining himself with the chess pieces, marching them around the board and sighing over the absence of his new friend.

Selina had her needlework and a growing feeling of dread. It was a lie to say she was waiting eagerly for his homecoming. But without his presence in it, the house seemed even larger and emptier than it had the day before. She did not belong here. Pretending she did put a strain on her nerves.

When he finally arrived, he came straight to the sitting room to join them, offering a deep bow to her and a smile to Edward, who looked at him hopefully, glancing to the chessboard and away as if afraid to ask for attention, lest his request be refused.

'It is rather late for that,' the Duke said. 'But...' He went to the drawer of a side table and pulled out a deck of cards and offered it to the boy with a smile.

Her son tipped his head to the side, considering. He was no more familiar with them than he had been with the chess set on the previous evening. The Duke was probably wondering what, if anything, the boy was allowed to do when in her care. And what, if anything, his father had taught him while the man was still alive.

The answer to the second question was close to nothing. She had not noticed it when they were alone together, but Edward seemed starved for male attention, soaking up the Duke's favour as a parched plant took in water.

Why did that man have to be so deceptively charming?

He was smiling as he dealt out the cards quickly to the two of them, as if he had been just as anxious to see Edward as the boy had him.

But why did it have to be this pastime? She had shielded Edward from his father's vice thus far and had no desire for him to take up the habit now. She looked up from her embroidery and gave a sniff of disapproval.

He ignored it and said to the boy, 'This game is deceptively simple. But you will discover, after a time, that it can be quite challenging.'

'Can Mama play as well?' Edward said, looking across at her with longing.

She gave a slight shake of her head and glared at the Duke.

'Perhaps another night, once you have learned the rules and she is not busy with her needlework,' he said, smiling to put the boy at ease. Then he went on to explain the rules.

The hour passed quietly, as Alex taught the boy casino and vingt-et-un and she sat on the other side of the room, stabbing her sampler and waiting for the night to be over, so that she could talk to the Duke without Edward hearing.

When he had kissed her goodnight and was gone from the room, she stared at Glenmoor, her eyes narrowed. 'I do not want you playing cards with my son.'

'My stepson, you mean,' he said, staring back at her with a placid smile. 'In time, you will see that there are things I can teach him that you, as his mother, will not know.'

'But those things will not include cards,' she said, equally firm.

He picked up the deck from off the table, fanned it effortlessly, then shuffled, his long fingers riffling through the cards with a dexterity that enthralled her.

'If you deny him this, you will create just the un-healthy fascination you seek to avoid. You are far more likely to turn him into his father than to keep him from travelling the particular path you most want him to avoid.'

'And what do you mean by that?' she said, know-ing perfectly well what he meant.

'There are card games that require luck and those that require skill. Your husband had neither luck nor skill, nor the intelligence to know the difference,' the Duke said, his smile disappearing.

'How dare you?' she said, eyes blazing.

'Speak ill of the dead?' he replied, setting the cards aside. 'I dare because, at least in this case, someone must. Your husband made many mistakes in life—the greatest of them was how he treated you and Edward. If he could not keep himself from gambling, the least he could have done was told you the truth and stayed alive to face the consequences of his losses. But he left you to do that, didn't he?'

'He did not know what he was doing,' she said softly, not wanting to be reminded of it.

'He knew exactly what he was doing,' he pressed. 'He left you a list of his debts. You told me so your-self.'

'In letters that were not addressed to you,' she countered, relieved that she could turn the argument back on to his faults and away from John's.

'You were willing to confess the truth to a man you had never met,' he reminded her. 'And to take money from him when it was offered.'

'I had no choice,' she replied, trying not to think of how desperate she had been in those first days.

'Because of your husband,' he reminded her. 'And what would you have done if I hadn't offered to help you? Would you have gone to Baxter, or some other man?'

It would have been that or the poorhouse. And wouldn't it have been better for Edward to have had some stability, even if it meant sacrificing herself and her pride? 'I went to you, which was bad enough,' she said, hoping to wound him.

'And you have again,' he reminded her.

'Because you forced me into this marriage.'

'Baxter forced you into it by revealing our arrangement.'

'You did, by your previous actions. If you hadn't meddled, there would have been no scandal,' she insisted.

'If you would have remarried someone else when I suggested it, there would have been no scandal either. But instead, you were waiting for an offer from Abbott.'

'I...' she said, unable to bring herself to deny the fact.

'And now that you have got one, you are not happy with it,' he declared. 'It was only me, all along. And you cannot abide that, can you?' He stared at her, his expression one part pity and one part frustration.

He reached for her then, taking her upper arms in the gentlest of grasps. 'You must understand why, in my letters, I was careful not to lead you on. I knew you would hate me when you learned who I was. I knew it was hopeless. I did not want to hurt you. But I could not stop writing.' His voice was rough, but soft. And now his hands stroked her arms, grazing the sides of her breasts.

At the slightest touch, she felt a growing yearning deep inside. Her body tingled and, without meaning to, she leaned into him, stepping closer.

He responded, his breath low and shaky. 'I could not leave you, even when I knew it was best for both of us. And now, here we are.' His arms wrapped around her, stroking her back as they had her arms, moving slowly from nape to the small of her back, where they settled, pressing, urging her close to nestle against his body.

It was wrong. But Lord, she wanted it. It had been so long since she'd been touched and he was so gentle, coaxing, not demanding, waiting for her to make the next move.

She took a breath and forced herself to forget who he was, tipping her head up to his and closing her eyes.

His lips met hers, surprising her with their hunger. He paused for only a moment before opening her mouth with a lick of his tongue, kissing her in a way meant to banish the last inhibition, his tongue teasing hers, bringing her to life until she could not help but kiss him back.

It was beyond good, like life itself pouring back into her with each stroke of his tongue. She balled her fists in his lapels, pressing herself into the solidness of his chest, breathing in the sweet, spicy scent of him and letting her mind drift. This was what she had wanted, when she'd read his letters, a strong man to lean upon. Someone who would hold her as if she meant the world to him.

One of his hands stole up to cup her breast through the fabric of her gown and she felt her nipples, already tight with desire, puckering, eager to be kissed. His other hand, which was still at the small of her back, slid lower, moulding her against the bulge of his erection.

If he wanted, he could have her here and she would not stop him. Even with closed eyes, she could picture him as he had been last night, large and naked and virile in a way that was nothing like John had been.

Then she remembered who he really was and the promise that she had exacted from him that their marriage would be cold and barren. She pulled away, out of his grasp, hurriedly patting her gown as if to assure herself that she was still decent. She felt naked before him, even though fully dressed.

He stared at her, panting, expectant. But he did not reach for her again.

'You should not have done that,' she said automatically.

'I?' he said with a sardonic raise of an eyebrow. 'I suppose now you will tell yourself that you were forced into it.'

He had not forced her; she had gone to him willingly and she hated her weakness. 'Whatever it was, it will not happen again,' she said, stepping back to put some space between them.

He was staring at her now, searching for…something; she was not sure what. He nodded, as if he'd found it, and said, 'You know that is not true. What will happen between us is inevitable. But when it happens, you will be the one to come to me.'

'Never,' she said, but the word had no real strength to it.

'Soon,' he replied, with even more certainty. 'The door to my room is unlocked, should you choose to use it. Goodnight, Selina.' And then he left her alone.

Chapter Fifteen

She'd let him kiss her. And it had been every bit as good as he'd hoped. Her lips were like honey, her response eager. And her body pressed against his had been the sweetest of tortures, hinting at a future that he didn't dare hope for.

But he did hope. He had been up most of the night, staring at the door that connected their rooms, willing her to open it and come to him. It had remained stubbornly closed. Eventually, he had fallen into a fitful sleep of erotic dreams and woken alone and disappointed.

But perhaps tonight would be different. They were to make their first public appearance as a married couple at the Folbroke ball, an invitation she had chosen to accept without his prompting. He hoped that meant she did not intend to embarrass him. It would be impossible to do so without shaming herself, and he did not want that. She might have married him out of spite, but he had more than enough love for both of them and did not want to see her hurt.

After a light breakfast, he went to the study and put daydreams aside in favour of the stack of bills that were accumulating on his desk. He had been there for nearly an hour before he noticed a shadow lurking in the doorway. He tried to ignore it, but after a few minutes gave up and called, 'Come.'

A moment more passed before the boy appeared, toeing the edge of the carpet, staring at Alex, as if considering.

'It's all right,' Alex said in a softer tone, gesturing him to come closer.

'Mother says I am not to bother you when you are working.'

'Then you do not have to worry. I will tell you when you are bothering me, and you are not.'

There was another moment of hesitation, then Edward stepped into the room and climbed up into the chair in front of the desk. He stared in silence at the papers stacked there and then back at Alex. 'What are you doing?'

'I am going over this month's bills for my estate.' Then he added, 'I have a house in the country that is much bigger than this with miles of land around it.' He thought for a moment, remembering the things about the property that had fascinated him when he had visited as a child. 'There is a stream for trout and many trees that are good for climbing, and a Roman ruin as well. Sometimes, I would find coins in the garden.'

The boy's eyes grew round with wonder. 'And can I go there?'

'We will all go there, once the Season is done.' At least, he assumed that they would. Perhaps his wife meant to remain in town as his mother used to, when she was avoiding her second husband. It would not hurt if he gained an ally in Edward, to encourage Selina to make the trip.

'I would like to see the ruins,' he said. 'And I will take the compass, so I do not get lost.' He patted his pocket.

'That is very wise,' Alex said, nodding in approval. Then he sobered. 'How much has your mother told you about our marriage, Edward?'

'That we were to come and live with you now and that you would be my...' he paused as if trying to remember the word '...my stepfather, which is not like a father at all.'

Alex stifled his wince. 'It is different, yes. But did she explain to you how?'

Edward shook his head.

'When I die, most of my property, the money, the title of Duke and the great house that we will live in will pass to my son, if I am blessed to have one.' Now was not the time to explain how unlikely that seemed right now. But he went on. 'It will not go to you, since you are my stepson and have, or had, a father of your own.'

'And he did not leave me anything,' Edward said with surprising bluntness.

'Should I pass, you will be taken care of,' Alex said hurriedly. 'I will set up a trust for you and, while I am alive, I will see to your welfare, your education and guide you to a career, if you wish to have one. Your father would have done the same, if he had not died when he did.'

Edward blinked at him, thinking. Then he announced, 'Father shot himself. My mother does not like to speak of it, but I heard the servants talking.'

'Did your mother tell you that I was with your father, the night he died?' He held his breath, afraid of the answer.

The boy solemnly shook his head.

'I played cards with him. He lost money to me,' Alex admitted. 'But when I played with him, I had no idea...' How was he to explain this? 'But it wasn't my fault that he died. Your father was a very unhappy man,' he stated.

'Why?' Edward said, a strange cloud passing over his face.

'Not because of anything you did,' he said hurriedly, and watched the boy slump in relief.

Had Selina really told the boy nothing? 'And not just because of the game he played with me. He was unlucky in cards. He lost all the money he had and was embarrassed to tell you.'

'We had to move houses,' Edward said with a frown.

'Because he lost the house to a man named Baxter,' Alex supplied.

'Mother was very sad,' he replied thoughtfully.

'I imagine she was.'

'And angry as well,' the boy said, still frowning.

'But never at you,' Alex assured him.

'At my father?' he said, his voice trembling a little.

'At the way things turned out,' Alex said, allowing himself a small lie. 'Life has been very difficult for her since your father died.'

'But it is better now,' Edward said, beaming at him. 'She has you to take care of her.'

'Of course,' Alex said, feeling the guilt rising in his throat like bile. He forced it back down again and added, 'I will take care of her.' Whether she wanted him to or not. 'We will take care of her together.'

Edward responded with a solemn nod. Then asked, 'What do I have to do?'

'Continue to do what you are doing,' Alex said, relieved to be back on solid ground. 'Keep up with your studies and obey her when she asks something of you. She is very proud of you and happy that you are with her. She has told me so herself.'

Edward nodded again, content with the answer, then stared at him as though afraid to ask his next question.

'And I am happy, too,' Alex said, watching the boy relax again. 'I do not have time for games today. But if you wish, you may sit in the chair by the window while I work.'

The boy climbed up into the seat, watching with interest as Alex returned to his accounts.

Selina stared into the mirror in her bedroom as her maid fastened the back of the new ball gown she had chosen for the night's outing. She'd made a special trip to Bond Street and begged the poor modiste to rush so that it might be ready for tonight's ball. And now, though she could not see anything wrong with the construction or trim, it seemed to be missing something.

The whole shopping trip had seemed rather strange to her, for she had never been in a position where money was no obstacle to the purchase of a gown. Of course the dress could be ready on such short notice for *Her Grace*. The seamstresses had thrown aside their other tasks for a chance to sew for a duchess. They had been excited to do so.

And if truth were told, Selina was excited as well. She had gone into the shop wondering if there might be some way to annoy Glenmoor with her purchases. John would have been appalled at the price she had paid for a single gown.

But Alex Conroy was nothing like her last husband. When she had remarked in passing that she would need new clothing for all the events he'd wished her to accept, he had simply nodded and told her to send the bills to his bank.

She had toyed with the idea of buying something ridiculous that would embarrass him, but hurriedly put the idea aside. If she made a cake of herself with too many ruffles, or garish colours, the gossips would announce that the new Duchess had no sense of fashion.

And, if she was honest with herself, she wanted to look beautiful, even if it was only for herself. There was no indication that her wearing grey to the wedding had insulted him. But it had made her feel shabby and elicited some odd looks from the Duchess of Fallon. She would not go through that again.

So now she was wearing emerald green silk, with a bodice cut dangerously low. Perhaps that was the problem with it. She had no jewellery to wear, beyond the jet brooch she'd worn after John died. And even on a green ribbon, the little cameo was inappropriate for evening.

Perhaps there was some piece of Glenmoor family jewellery she could borrow for the night, so she might not look so plain. But that would require her asking her husband for his help and nothing could induce her to do so. It would be hard enough to walk at his side tonight without knowing that she was even deeper in his debt.

Then there was a knock on the bedroom door. When her maid opened it, His Grace's valet handed her a blue leather case, delivered with His Grace's compliments.

She could not help the gasp of shock when she opened it. It was a parure, complete with necklace, hairpins, ear-drops and shoe clips. Gold leaves and stems intertwined, ending in a complicated arrangement of floral sprigs where each blossom was set with an emerald at its centre.

She should refuse it. She had sworn, when she decided to marry Glenmoor, that it was only to spite him at every turn. But she could not bring herself to close the case, much less send it away.

Her maid had even fewer scruples and removed the necklace from the case, draping it around her throat and fastening the clasp at the back. 'Oh, madam. I mean, Your Grace. It is perfect. Sit down and let me do up your hair with the pins.'

Selina sank into the chair at the vanity table and watched as Molly put up her hair. The girl was right. It suited the dress perfectly.

You are stunning in green.

The words popped into her head, seemingly out of nowhere. Then she remembered them from one of Abbott's letters, received after the Fallon ball. She had been so excited to think that he had seen her there. And all along, it had been Glenmoor, flattering her and forcing his way into her company.

But then, she touched the necklace at her throat and wondered aloud, 'How did he know?'

Molly giggled. 'He asked me what you would be wearing. He said the family jewels were hopelessly out of style and that there was no time to reset them. So he bought something new that would suit you.'

'Oh.' She went back to staring in the mirror as Molly curled her hair and then piled it high on her head. What was she to do about this latest development? She should thank her husband for the gift. But she had not asked for it, nor did she like the idea that she was beholden to him in this new and surprising way.

But it was strangely touching to see a necklace glittering at her throat, after a year with nothing there. Even when she'd had jewels, they had been simple ones: a strand of pearls and an amber cross that had belonged to her mother.

John had promised to drape her in diamonds, when he was courting her. But even then, she'd known that he was exaggerating. After they were married, the promised gifts had never materialised. If there was money to spare for luxuries, it had been lost at the gaming tables. Afterwards, there was always a promise that next month, or next year, when he was winning, everything would be different.

She shook her head, trying to escape the memory, only to receive a frustrated sigh from Molly, who was affixing the last of the pins to her curls. John was gone and she needn't think about the unhappy times in her past.

Things were better now.

The fact hit her like a slap. It was undeniable that the last year, she had been happier than she had been with John. There had been no worries about money, no loneliness and no broken promises.

Then she remembered the enormous lie that her whole life had balanced upon. Perhaps things had not been better. Perhaps Glenmoor had only found a different way to hurt her. The parure was a peace offering, trying to make up for that. And, she had to admit, it was an impressive one.

She must not allow herself to be bought. If their relationship was only about money, she was no better than the newspapers said she was. She would wear the thing because it suited the dress and because pulling the pins from her hair would make unnecessary work for Molly.

But she would not allow the presence of a few stones to change who she was. She would not be in awe of the thing, or of the man who gave it to her. She would be true to herself tonight, whatever that turned out to be.

Molly was finished with her hair and Selina rose and turned towards the door. After a final brush to the folds of her skirt, she went out into the hall to find her husband.

Chapter Sixteen

Alex was waiting at the foot of the stairs when Selina appeared at their head, and he allowed himself a moment to admire her.

She was magnificent. The jewels he had bought her were a perfect match to the green of her gown; her skin was luminous beneath the gold, glowing pink and flushed with an excitement that she could not conceal.

She did not smile when she looked at him, but that was not unusual. At least she did not look haughty. He did not think he could abide having the kind of duchess his mother had been. That woman had been arrogant in the extreme, aware of her power and not above using it against people she felt were inferior to her.

In contrast, Selina looked elegant but approachable. She had reached him now and he took her hand, relieved that she did not pull away from him as he escorted her to the carriage and helped her to her seat. She was quiet, which was also not unusual. She rarely spoke to him when she did not have to.

But tonight, it felt different, as if there was something she wished to say that she could not manage.

He understood the feeling. There were frequently things he could not manage to say to her, although conversing had grown somewhat easier since their marriage. Perhaps it was because they were so frequently arguing. And why was it easier to find words for that?

He smiled.

She noticed and was unable to help a small sound of enquiry.

'I was thinking that we are often sniping at each other when we are home. I hope we shall not do it tonight,' he said in explanation.

'I hope you do not give me cause,' she said, still unsmiling.

'I am not planning anything unusual,' he said. 'We must share a dance, of course. But I do not mean to monopolise your time. This evening is for you as much as for me, and many people will wish to congratulate you on your recent marriage.'

'Oh.' She sounded small, which wasn't like her. Was she worried about being a focus of attention?

'There will be a stir about you in the papers, tomorrow. For when is there not gossip about someone bagging a title?'

'I thought we married to prevent gossip,' she said with a sigh.

'Perhaps if you'd married some minor lord, that would be true,' he said. 'But a duchess cannot avoid notice.'

Now she looked nervous, but said nothing.

'Do not worry,' he said quickly. 'They will find no fault with you. You are…' Now his words were starting to fail him again. He looked away, out the window of the carriage so that he did not become confused. 'You are a goddess. Men will be clamouring for your attention. And women will flock to befriend you.'

There was a pause as she absorbed the words. Then she muttered, 'Thank you.' And added, 'And thank you for the gift of the necklace.' The words seemed to come grudgingly, but they were there all the same and more than he'd expected from her.

'You are most welcome. You deserved some sort of wedding gift.'

'People might have wondered,' she declared.

'That is not why I did it,' he replied. He had been almost childishly eager to give her something, to prove himself worthy of her. It was disappointing to think she felt it was only from obligation.

They arrived at the Folbroke residence and he helped her down from the carriage, doing his best to ignore the weight of her hand on his arm and the warmth of her body beside his. She was rarely this near to him for long and he savoured the moment, keeping her close as he introduced her to the Earl and his Countess.

Then he led her to the dance floor. 'Will you join me?' It was nothing more than a country dance. But he thought that, if she allowed him this, perhaps he could convince her to save him the waltz later.

They moved through the steps, bowing and weav-

ing among the others in their set, advancing and re-
treating as the music called them to do.

She smiled at him. Nervously at first, then with
more feeling as the spirit of the dance took hold of her.
Perhaps she was happy. Or perhaps it was merely too
much work to remember to scowl at him and smile at
the other men in the row.

Either way, he had the pleasure of looking at her,
of touching her hand and of watching her body as she
moved. Was this what courtship would have been,
had she allowed him one? Sighing over each smile
she imparted and waiting for the next brush of her
fingers against his?

The music ended all too soon and he walked her
back to the side of the room, procuring her a glass
of champagne and holding his breath as she allowed
him to tie the dance card to her wrist. Then, when he
could think of no other reason to remain at her side, he
bowed and said, 'If that is all, my dear, I cede the room
to you. I will be in the card room, if you need me.'

'The card room,' she said in a shocked voice, her
smile disappearing. 'You certainly will not.'

He dipped his head to hers so they might seem
more like a bride and groom and less like a fractious
couple about to argue in public. 'It is either that or
spend all my time with you. If you do not want me
playing cards, I will dance every dance with you and
hang on your every word. Does that suit you better?'

She hesitated for a moment, and he wondered if her
hatred of cards was even greater than her hatred of
him. Then she stepped away and made a vague ges-

ture in the direction of the hallway. 'Go if you must. But when you lose, do not come to me for the money to pay your creditors.' Without thinking, she touched her necklace as if fearing that he might take it away at the end of the night.

'I never lose,' he said with a smile. Then, before she could pull away, he kissed her quickly on the lips and left for the card room.

When he arrived, Evan was already there, taking in a hand of loo between dances. He slid his chair to the side to make room. Then, to his dismay, Baxter took a seat opposite them, offering an unctuous smile. 'Shall we play, gentlemen?'

Alex glanced around the room, considering and rejecting the possibility of finding a chair at a different table. Then he said, 'Since there is no good way to avoid it, I suppose we shall.'

Baxter laughed at the insult and helped himself to the deck, dealing out the cards. 'It is either that or one of us must go out and dance with your wife,' he suggested. 'But I suppose she is used to being abandoned for games of chance.'

'She will be glad of it, once she learns that I spared her your company,' Alex said, picking up his cards.

The play proceeded and, unlike most nights, the game would not go his way. He began to regret his glib comment to Selina about always winning. Things went no better for Evan and they watched pot after pot going to Baxter.

When Alex's purse was empty, he pushed away from the table and made to leave.

'So soon?' said Baxter, grinning.

'I am played out,' Alex said, trying to hide his annoyance at his bad luck.

'You needn't stop. I am willing to take your marker.' He paused and then said, 'Your word is good, isn't it?'

Alex felt his temper rising and was ready to retort that his honour was not a matter of question. Then he remembered whom he was talking to and reined in his temper.

Loo was not the only game Baxter was playing. Each word and action he offered was meant to elicit a predicted response from the other players. There was something in the manner of the man before him that seemed too confident in the outcome of the game and the reactions of his opponents. If Alex wished to best him, he should not be playing along.

So he smiled and pushed away from the table. 'Unlike some men, I know my limits.'

'Unlike John Ogilvie, perhaps,' Baxter said, staring up at him. 'You were much slower to end the game the night he died, weren't you?'

Another taunt. To what purpose? Alex stared back at him, wondering. 'I am beginning to see why so many people owe you money, Baxter. But I am not going to be one of them. And now, if you will excuse me, they are tuning up for the waltz and I must go and find my wife.'

In the ballroom, Selina sipped her lemonade, curling her toes in her slippers to stretch her tired feet.

'How do you like being a duchess?' Mary Wilson asked, from a seat at her side.

'Very well,' Selina said, trying to ignore the pang of guilt she felt at the admission. Now that she had the protection of her husband's title, her glass and dance card were full and everyone in the room seemed eager to greet her, meet her and be her friend. 'I must not allow my head to be turned by flattery,' she added, 'for there has been more than a little of that. I suppose I shall see what people really think of me, in tomorrow's papers…'

Mary laughed. 'Do not read them. You should know by now that the tattle sheets print nothing but nonsense.'

'Probably true,' she replied, still doubting. They certainly would not print the truth about her marriage for they did not know how she truly felt about the Duke. Even she was not sure of that, any more.

'And here comes your husband,' Mary said, nudging her and grinning. 'Is he not the handsomest man in the room?'

'You say that about any man with a title,' Selina said with a laugh. Even so, she could not help the way her heart lurched at the sight of Glenmoor, who was resplendent in a dark blue evening coat and buff breeches.

'Do you feel differently about him, now that you are married?' Mary whispered from behind her fan.

'I…' Selina stared at him as he approached, trying to decide how to answer the question. Then she remembered that he was on his way back from the card room and her resolve stiffened. 'I do not wish to speak of it.'

'Of course not, Your Grace,' Mary replied in a hurt tone.

She turned to apologise, but it was too late, for her husband had arrived at their side. As usual, he was courtesy itself to Mary, bowing over her hand and smiling. 'Mrs Wilson,' he said, as if greeting an old friend. 'I hope you don't mind that I have come to claim my wife for the waltz.'

Then he turned to Selina and gave her a smile different from the one she had received at home. Tonight, he was brilliant and flirtatious, playing the part of the gallant young lover and inviting her to play along for the sake of the crowd. 'If, that is, her card is not already full.'

She did not have to look at her dance card to know that the waltz had remained empty. The eager men who had sought her out for other dances had left that space free as if they'd known the Duke would be back for it. She smiled at Mary then, rose and turned to Glenmoor, offering her hand. 'Of course, Your Grace.' Then she allowed him to lead her out on to the dance floor.

It was easier than it had been the first time they'd waltzed together, as this time there was no fear of his touch.

It should not be so. She should have resisted or refused his request. She might have claimed to be too tired and no one would have questioned it. Hadn't her plan been to fight him in all things?

But she liked dancing with him. Surely allowing herself this small pleasure was not a surrender? If she closed her eyes and let the music take her, being with him was like walking on air.

He let out a soft laugh and whispered, 'Pretending that I am someone else?'

She opened her eyes again, her smile faltering as did her step.

He caught her and brought her back to the rhythm with his body. 'We move well together, whether you want us to or not. I do not think we can help it. We are alike, Selina, mated in all the ways that matter.' Then he added, 'All the ways but one.'

The reminder sent a tremor through her, like the ring of crystal when the rim was struck. She did not want to feel this answering chime and the tingle of desire that came with it. This wanting to know what it would be like to be with him and what they would be like together. Would it be like dancing?

'Remember,' he said softly, 'the door is unlocked. It is only your stubbornness that keeps it closed.'

'I am not stubborn,' she said, latching on to the only thing she dared comment over.

'Of course not,' he said, his voice like velvet against her frayed nerves. 'You are merely resolved. But I knew that about you from your letters. You have needed to be strong to survive. But it is not a weakness to change your mind.'

Before she could think of an answer, the dance had ended and he was leading her back to her chair and relinquishing her to her next partner, who stood ready for the Sir Roger de Coverley. Her mind was whirling as she danced and, without meaning to, her eyes searched the room for Glenmoor, whenever she turned.

He was standing to the side, talking with his brother, Fallon. And often, when she looked to him, his eyes met hers as if she was never far from his thoughts. She looked away again, trying to remember the promises she had made to herself, and to John. And for a time, she was resolved.

But then the ball was over and Glenmoor collected her again, still painfully polite, but somehow, more confident than he had been before. He led her to the carriage, helped her up into it and took the seat across from her, stretching his legs out before him. 'Did you enjoy the evening, my dear?'

'I am not your dear,' she said automatically.

He ignored the retort and said, 'Is that a yes, or a no?'

'It was very pleasant,' she said in a more polite tone.

'I am glad,' he said, then turned to stare out the window, allowing her to ride in silence. Strangely, this was even more difficult than talking to him. There was a tension between them that was different than before.

In previous trips, she'd felt wariness, and repulsion. It had been easier to keep her distance and remain apart from him. But now there was a magnetic pull drawing her eyes to his face, his body, his hands, his lips. It was probably the flush of excitement, having danced all evening and drunk too much champagne. Tonight, she had not been someone's mother, or someone's widow. She'd been a wife. And, though she was not sure how such evenings ended for others, she knew what her imagined ending might be.

But not with him. Never with him.

Someone like him, perhaps. Someone tall and handsome and polite. Someone who smiled at her and danced with her as if he already knew her body and what it would take to pleasure it.

They arrived home and he was as solicitous there as he had been at the ball. He waited at the doorway for her to pass and slipped the cloak from her shoulders, allowing his fingers to brush the skin of her throat as he did so.

Then they went upstairs to their respective bedrooms, calling for servants and preparing for bed. But when her maid left her, she did not feel truly alone, knowing that he was there, just on the other side of the unlocked door, waiting for her.

The feelings she had for him were purely physical and there was no way to control that. Perhaps what some people said about widows was true and they were too knowledgeable to ever be truly proper. When she was a green girl, she certainly would not have had the nerve to peek in at him as she had done on the first night, to catch a glimpse of his nakedness. Nor would she have known what to do with what she had seen.

Of course, even clothed, he was a formidable sight.

There was something about the quirk of the corner of his mouth that fascinated her. It was as if he was aware of what his lips could do to her after that interlude in the sitting room and the thought amused him to an almost smile.

Or he might have been thinking of something else entirely and the idea of carnal bliss might be totally in her own mind. That was why she could not stop looking at his hands. She could imagine those hands on her breasts, squeezing until her breath caught in her throat. And one of his long legs hooking casually over her hip to pull her close as he entered her.

She sat up in bed, hands twisting nervously in the sheets. If she closed her eyes, she could almost feel him moving inside her. It was better if her eyes were closed, for she could forget who it was she was thinking of, forget where she was and who she was and who she had been, and focus only on the pretended sensation of a man hard for her, taking her.

That was what she had done for Abbott, after all. She had read his letters before bed and used her imagination for the rest. And for a time, that had been enough.

Her eyes popped open again and she stared at the door, just a few feet away. It didn't have to be a dream. She could have what she wanted, if she had the nerve to open the door and walk through. It did not have to mean anything more than the scratching of an itch. It was not as if it would mean more to him than that. It never did, to a man.

She needn't fear rejection. He had made it very clear

that she was welcome in his bed. She just had to go and present herself and nature would take its course.

She threw back the covers and swung her feet out of the bed, shivering in the night air for a moment, feeling her breasts tighten with the chill and, surprisingly, with anticipation.

Then she walked towards the door, grasped the handle and paused for only a moment before throwing it open and walking into the Duke's room.

Chapter Seventeen

He was lying on the bed with a book in his lap, the sheet draped at his waist and his bare chest exposed, oblivious to the coolness of the room. At her appearance, he looked up from his reading, not so much surprised as curious. His head tipped to the side, considering, but he said nothing, simply waited for her to explain herself.

She wished she could oblige, but her mind was blank. The sight of him rendered her mute. He was even more formidable up close than he had been in the peek she had taken through the keyhole, his upper body well-muscled, his chest flat and hard in a way that made her fingers ache to touch it. And the memory of what lay still hidden beneath the sheet...

She wondered if she was quite right in the head. Surely women were not supposed to be the aggressors in the bedroom. She had never been before. But since it seemed he was a man of his word, he made no move to rise and help her. She would have to be the one to start this, just as he had said.

She took a step forward, into the room, and undid the buttons of her nightgown, shrugging out of it and stepping clear as it dropped to the floor.

His only response was a raised eyebrow and a tensing of muscle as his breathing increased. Then, slowly, he closed the book in his lap and set it to the side.

What had she expected? An announcement giving her permission to continue? Or perhaps she had hoped he would send her away. There was no sign of either. He was letting her decide what was to come next and she knew what she wanted that to be.

She walked to the bedside and slid the sheet down his hips and out of the way. Then she drank in the sight of him, bare and still before her, waiting. But not unresponsive this time, for he grew aroused beneath her gaze, unable to hide his interest in her.

In an act of supreme courage, she reached for him, tightening her hand around his manhood and stroking it to full erection. His breath quickened now and he shifted on the bed, reaching for her.

She stepped clear of his hands, not ready to feel his touch in response. She did not want to be coddled and held, to have him turn this into something that she knew it was not. She longed for something base and primal. She wanted release.

She took a breath and stepped forward again, batting his hands out of the way.

He deliberately folded them behind his head, leaning back into the pillows to watch her touching him. His breath hissed between his teeth as she stroked, but the pace of each exhalation was carefully controlled, as if he did not want to admit to what was happening to him, lest it cause her to stop.

He was hard beneath her fingers and she was aroused by the sight of him, wet with anticipation of their joining. She climbed on to the bed, straddling his hips, pressing him tightly against her belly before smoothing the single drop that had formed at the tip down his shaft. Then she slid forward and rose up, hovering over him for a moment before easing down to take him into her body.

'Hell's teeth.' The exclamation slipped out of his mouth and then he was silent again, closing his eyes and then opening them slowly, as if he expected she might vanish if he looked away.

She pursed her own lips, refusing to explain or apologise, or, worst of all, to lean forward for a kiss. She did not want tenderness. She wanted the hard, tight, full feeling that she had now and the mad rush of sensation as she began to move on him.

He seemed to sense what she needed, for when he reached for her again, it was to seize her hips to steady himself as he thrust, finding the rhythm she had set and matching it.

She gasped as he pushed into her and again at the retreat and return, and the commanding pressure of his fingers on her flesh.

'Is this what you want?' he murmured on another thrust. 'To be taken hard? To be used, as you are using me?'

A week ago, she would have whimpered and rolled passively on to her back, afraid to admit the truth.

But then, she had not been married to her enemy and fighting these strange uncontrollable desires. Tonight, she closed her eyes and bit her lip, bucking her hips, grinding down on to him and letting him fill her.

'Very well, then,' he muttered, and drew back and took her again, even deeper.

She gasped and steadied herself as he thrust again and again. Her thoughts scattered, fear and disgust and sadness all fled until there was nothing left but the pounding of her heart and the pounding of his body into hers, demanding her surrender and release.

She tried to hold back, to make it last, but her reserve shredded like silk and she panted like an animal, shaking with the orgasm that tore through her as he finished with a curse and one last plunge into the depths of her.

The passion ebbed and they stilled, but did not relax. She was still trembling like a bowstring, ready to go again. It had been good in the way she wanted and better than anything she'd experienced in years. But there was the nagging sense that it could be so much more, if only she was willing for it to be so.

Sensing her hesitation, he sighed and withdrew, rolled away from her to take up his book again as if nothing had happened.

Perhaps nothing had. She had got what she wanted. What reason was there to remain? Refusing to be hurt by it, she climbed out of the bed and returned to her room.

Chapter Eighteen

It was an excellent morning.

Alex smiled down the table to the footman at the door of the dining room, overwhelmed with good humour. If he was honest, it was not the best possible of mornings. If it had been that, he would still be in bed, staring at the sex-tousled hair of his wife, spread across the pillows, tickling his arms as he pulled her close to wake her and take her.

There had been no romance in their joining, no wooing or ceremony. She had not come to him to be loved. He supposed he should be hurt by that fact, for he wanted more from her than a purely physical union. He wanted the joining of spirits that he'd felt in the letters they'd exchanged.

But it was hard to feel pain over what had happened when she had delivered pleasure in such an effective, no-nonsense way. God bless a woman who knew her own mind. She had taken him in her hand, worked him to the point of desperation and then provided the relief of her body, gasping out her own climax as he'd found his.

If the act had not left him spouting poetry and cloud-headed, it had certainly left him to sleep soundly and to rise with the urge to crow like a rooster, to announce to the whole world that he was King and had claimed his Queen.

There was the slight problem that his Queen did not want to be claimed. But she had brought that on herself by opening the door of his bedroom and climbing into his bed. She was regretting it this morning, by the look on her face as she sat across the dining table from him. It was unusually sour, as if daring him to mention their intimacy.

'Chocolate?' he said, lifting the pot and gesturing to her cup.

'Thank you.' The words were mundane, but icy.

Alex smiled back and handed the pot across the table to Selina.

Their fingers brushed on the handle and she withdrew her hand as if the contact had burned.

It was not the adoring sigh he might have wished for, but it was proof that she was not indifferent to him. She might not like that she felt something, but she felt it all the same.

He nodded and withdrew as well, ceding her the pot and watching as she poured it herself.

He wondered what she had made of what they had done. Women did not feel things in the same way as men, or so he had been told. But perhaps this one did. She had been hungry enough to come to his room.

There was no point in speculating if she would not talk. But it would have been nice to receive a letter from her today, telling him what she had really thought of the ball and what had happened after. She had not been afraid to speak the truth to Abbott, nor had she been angry at him for things he could not control.

As for Alex? He was going to read the newspaper and try to pretend that he did not want to lean over the table to kiss his wife good morning. He flicked open the pages, turning directly to the tattle page to see what had been said about the previous evening.

He scanned down the page and could not prevent an exclamation of shock when he found what he was looking for.

Selina startled like a frightened deer. 'What?'

'Nothing,' he said quickly, closing the paper again.

'Is it about me?' she said, reaching for it. 'Let me see.'

'No.' But that had been a foolish response. If she did not see it now, with him here, she would simply find it later when he had left the table. He took a breath and handed the paper across the table to her. 'The things that they publish are mostly rubbish. It is best to ignore them.'

Last night at the Earl of F.'s ball, bystanders were shocked to watch the Duke of G. lose a large sum of money to B.B. That man once took the house of Mr O. in a similar game, the first husband of G.'s lovely new bride. Does history repeat itself for the poor Duchess?

'You said you would win,' she said, looking up from the paper.

'I do not always. That is why it is called gambling,' he replied.

'I did not want you to go into that room.'

'Nor did you want me to stay with you,' he reminded her. 'And it is not all bad. They called you lovely, which you are.'

She growled in frustration.

He shrugged and added, 'And it was not a substantial sum. He took as much as I'd planned to wager for the night, then I left the table. I am not beholden to him in any way, as so many men seem to be.' He considered for a moment. 'Although he seemed to be eager for me to get in over my head.'

'Because he still thinks to have me,' she said with a shudder.

'Then he is a fool,' Alex said. 'I told him what would happen to him if he bothered you again.'

'And when did you do that? Or is that something that I will have to read in the papers, too?'

He sighed, for it seemed that he could do nothing right as it pertained to the woman he had married. 'I went to him before the wedding and told him he had lost and to go away.'

'As if I was the prize in a contest?' she said.

'Not at all in that way,' he said, regretting his words. 'I sought to protect you.'

'I thought that marrying you would do that,' she said, looking as frustrated as he felt.

'So did I,' he admitted. 'But it seems I will have to make good on my threat to him.'

'And how will you do that?' she said, her eyes narrowing, then added, 'And do not tell me you will duel. Letting blood might salve your wounded pride, but it would do nothing to help me at all.'

'For a moment, I thought you might be worrying for my safety,' he said, irritated.

She stared back at him, unflinching, waiting for a better solution.

And what would that be? When he had made the threat to keep Baxter away from her, he had thought that the words would be enough and had made no plan. That was his first mistake, but he would not make another.

He thought for a moment more and an idea came to him, but he immediately rejected it, for he was sure Selina would never approve or agree. But the thought would not leave him and he could not begin to persuade her if he did not voice it.

He gave her what he hoped was a winning smile and said, 'On our wedding day, I suggested we have a ball. But I think we should have a card party instead.'

'We most certainly will not,' she said, pushing away from the table and him.

'There is no better way to show that we are not afraid of Baxter and the things that the papers might say about us,' he said.

'But I am afraid,' she replied, her angry façade crumbling to reveal her true feelings. Her grey eyes were huge in her pale face and her lip trembled as if tears might be imminent.

He reached out a hand to cover hers. 'There will be nothing like your husband's gaming. I promise. The stakes will be low and I will eject anyone who is bidding outrageously.'

'John made promises to me as well,' she said, staring at him doubtfully.

'I am not John,' he said gently. 'I have never had a problem with cards.'

'Until the night you gamed with John,' she reminded him.

He took a breath and nodded. 'But though you blame me for what happened, there was nothing I did that caused his death. I happened to be the final straw in the heavy load he carried. But it could just as easily have been someone else.'

'And now you could be the bane of someone else,' she said, her frown returning.

'Baxter,' he reminded her. 'The man is a demon with a deck of cards and I mean to discover why. And to do that, I need to play him in my house, on my terms.'

'I am familiar with that madness,' she said, shaking her head. 'One game will become a dozen and will not end until he has fleeced you of everything you have.'

'One night will be enough,' he swore. 'If I fail, I will not ask you for more.'

She was hesitating now, as if she wanted to believe him. It gave him hope.

'Trust me,' he said, softly, urgently.

Those two words were a mistake greater than any he had made this morning. Her resolve returned and she smiled and shook her head. 'You are the last person in the world who should ask that of me.'

He wanted to remind her that she had awarded him with the ultimate act of trust, just the night before. But that would escalate the argument and do nothing to help his cause. Instead, he shrugged. 'As I promised, I will only ask this of you once. But I will have this game. Let me know when you have picked a date.'

She rose and pushed back from the table, her fists balled in frustration. 'Very well, Your Grace. It is obvious that I cannot stop you from ruin. But do not expect me to mourn you when you end up as John did.'

Selina hurried away, not wanting to hear another word of her husband's cloth-brained plan. If she'd had any hopes going into this marriage, it had been that her days of being a widow to a deck of cards were over. Her last marriage had ended long before John had died. His love of the game had killed anything that there had been between them.

Now the Duke meant to go the same way. She had not wanted him to duel, but she might have forgiven him for it, had he shot Baxter dead.

Of course, she did not mean to forgive him for everything. But then, she had not meant to go to his bed either. And even after doing that, she had not meant to be as affected by that experience as she'd been. She'd been seeking release, nothing more than that.

She had got that and returned to her bed. Then she'd dreamed. Whispered words of love. A man's arms about her. His lips kissing her hair. Flashes of sensation, glimpses of skin. The scent of sandalwood. She had woken feeling not just sated, but loved. It had frightened her.

But not as much as the suggestion of a card party. That was madness.

As she arrived at her room, ready to go in and slam the door, she heard the voice of her son from the nursery, reciting his Latin verbs for the governess whom the Duke had hired, in one of his more sensible moments. The ordinary sound calmed her nerves. Her fears were her own and she would not let them touch the boy in the nursery schoolroom.

She walked down the hall to him and stood at the open door of the room, soaking up the peace of it, exchanging satisfied smiles with the governess, Miss Gates.

Then Edward noticed her and stopped his declension, calling, 'Mama', and rushing to her side for the hug which she was eager to give him.

'My dear,' she responded. 'Well done. Are you enjoying your studies?'

He smiled and nodded, then cast a hesitant look at Miss Gates and requested, in his most formal voice, to be allowed to speak to his mother alone.

The governess nodded back and left the room, giving them their privacy, and Selina took one of the chairs at the schoolroom table, then gestured to Edward to join her, waiting for what he had to say.

'Mama,' he said in a cautious tone. 'Is it wrong that I like it here?'

'Not at all,' she said, relieved that this was their only problem.

'Because I think you do not.' His brow furrowed as he examined her face, searching for clues to her mood.

'Why do you say that?' she said, worried.

'Just now, you were arguing with the Duke,' he said.

She had been unaware that their voices had carried above stairs and wondered how many of her sharp comments he had heard in the last weeks. It made her ashamed.

'It is an adjustment for me, nothing more than that,' she assured him, wondering if that were true. 'Things will be different with time.'

'Because I like it better than I did at our old house,' he said firmly.

'That is what we promised you, when we first brought you here,' she said.

'And is it wrong that I like the Duke better than Father?'

This was a question that she had not expected. One that she did not know how to answer. She remained silent and allowed Edward to continue.

'I do not remember Father very well,' he said. 'He has been gone a long time.'

'A year,' Selina corrected, then remembered that for a child, twelve months was forever.

'And when he was not dead, I did not see him very often. I do not think he liked me very much.'

'Of course he liked you,' Selina said automatically, trying to think of an example she should give him. 'He was very proud when you were born.' And he had been.

Then she remembered her husband's words.

'Thank God it is not a girl.'

Perhaps pride was an overstatement. But John was dead and not all his words or ideas needed to live on in either of their memories. She gave her son an encouraging smile, trying not to think of how dismissive John had been of the idea that they might have a second child and his uninterest in spending time with her or their son. Nothing could compare to the lure of cards.

At last, she said, 'Your father was a troubled man. It did not always leave him time for his family.'

Edward gave her a knowing nod. 'But the Duke does not have troubles, does he?'

Of course he didn't. When he played, he usually won. And when he did not, he was eager for another game, just as John had been. Hopefully his pockets were deep enough to stand the madness he seemed eager to bring down on them. 'No, he does not,' she said, hoping that it was not another lie.

Edward smiled. 'That is good. Because I would not want to lose him like we did Father.'

'We will not lose him,' she said, and forced herself to give him an encouraging smile. 'We are a family now.' But was that true?

After last night, they were at least as much of a family as she and John had been. Perhaps more so, since the Duke seemed more interested in Edward's well-being than the boy's own father had been.

Edward seemed satisfied by her answers and called for his governess to come back, ready to continue his lessons.

Selina thanked the girl and left the room, still confused. Wasn't this what she wanted for her son? To see him happy and thriving?

Of course it was. But she had not expected to see him adjust so quickly or so well. Nor did she expect to feel the emotional ground shifting beneath her feet each time she was near Glenmoor. It had been easier to hate him unconditionally, as she had when she'd married him. But her feelings last night had been something else entirely. He had made her angry again at breakfast, but after talking to Edward, she did not know what to think.

She went to her room and shut the door, both relieved and frustrated to be alone. Then, the desk by the window caught her eye and she went to it, searching the drawers for paper and pen and sitting down to write.

Dear Abbott,

She shook her head at the madness of writing a letter to a man who did not exist. But she could not help the comfort she felt as the words describing the last weeks poured out of her and with them all the confusion and anger and fear.

*In my heart, I know this is no different from
writing to myself. But I cannot help it, my love.*
    I miss you.
    I need you.
    Tell me what I am to do.
Yours always,
Selina

Then she folded, addressed and sealed the letter,
kissed it once and threw it on to the desk.

Chapter Nineteen

Alex went to his study after breakfast, but left the door open so he might hear when Selina came back downstairs. He wanted to offer something in the way of an apology. He could have told her last night about the loss to Baxter, but had not thought it would matter, to her or to anyone else.

But that was what he'd thought on the night he'd won money from John Ogilvie. Somehow the gossips had made that into a major happening as well. And after seeing it in the papers, she had believed every word of it.

He smiled. The next time she read of him, it would be different. But first, she must be persuaded to accept the unacceptable and allow gambling in their home. And before that, he would have to coax her back downstairs. It appeared that she meant to spend the day in her room, hiding from him.

She avoided him at supper as well, having a tray sent up. But that night, they were to attend a musicale together, and he was relieved to see her appear at the foot of the stairs promptly at seven, in a white-and-gold evening gown, hair bedecked with some of the emeralds he had given her.

He raised her hand to his lips as he helped her into the carriage. 'You are lovely, as always.'

She blinked at him, face expressionless save for a faint blush staining her cheeks. 'Thank you.'

'And I am sorry I upset you this morning,' he added.

At this, she could not hide her look of surprise and, for a moment, her fingers tightened on his hand in what he hoped was gratitude.

'The amount I lost was a trifle and I did not think it would concern you. But you should not have read about it in the papers. I should have told you.'

'That is all right,' she said mechanically. The words sounded like a lie, but they were better than the alternative of a public row, so he accepted them with a smile.

'And as for the card party...'

'I do not wish to speak of it now,' she said.

They rode the rest of the way in silence.

When they arrived at the home of the Duchess of Danforth, they were ushered into the music room and seated side by side on the tightly packed chairs to hear a mediocre soprano warbling through a song about lost love.

Alex was usually immune to sentimentality, tolerating such performances rather than enjoying them.

But perhaps his feelings had been changed by marriage. Tonight, he found himself moved by the plight of the singer, hoping that the last verse would end in a reunion.

Or perhaps it was just the touch of his wife's arm that made him think of romance. She was close at his side, the bare skin above her long gloves brushing against his coat sleeve. Was it his imagination or was she deliberately leaning into him as she swayed to the music? Her eyes were closed as she lost herself in the song.

When it ended, she looked up at him, surprised at their nearness, and tried to correct her posture so they were no longer in contact. But the seats were so close together that there was no room for her to get away. After bumping against the gentleman on her other side, she shrugged and returned to leaning on Alex, nervous but resigned.

He smiled back at her, unperturbed. She might not admit the fact, but she was coming to accept him as her husband and to enjoy his company. It was like watching a plant growing, inch by inch. If he was patient, he would be rewarded by blooms.

In time, she would forgive him for the incident with her husband and forget the supreme mistake that Abbott had been, and they would have the marriage he had always hoped to share with her. But for now, they could sit together, as close as lovers. It was another hour and a half before the music ended and he escorted her back to the carriage for the quiet ride home.

* * *

Once there, they readied for bed. After checking on Edward, Selina called for her maid and sat in silence as Molly combed and braided her hair, still amazed at the changes that had happened in a few short weeks. Tonight's outing was one she'd never have been invited to, had she not married Glenmoor. The company had been august, the house grand, the refreshments elegant. The music had been sweet and sad and it had suited her mood.

It was not at all what she had imagined when she'd wanted to marry the mysterious Abbott. If she was honest, her thoughts on their life together had not strayed much further than the bedroom door. Once the lights had been out, there had been no need for talking. They'd understood each other perfectly. It had all been quite different than the awkward silences she shared with her husband, when she was never sure what he was thinking.

There certainly had not been other people in that fantasy. Nor had she needed to dress in fine clothes and act charming only to have her every move dissected and mocked in the papers the next day.

She missed the dream.

After writing to him this morning, she'd retrieved the stack of his letters that she had saved in her empty jewel case, pulling one from the ribbon-tied bundle and reading a random paragraph. Here, he was assuring her that Edward would be fine and that he had survived his own father's death, though his mother had not been nearly as caring as Selina was. Since he had become a duke, survival was an understatement and any similarities with Edward were hard to imagine.

In another he wrote that he had never owned a horse and much preferred to walk. It was a simple detail about his life, a casual admission that told much. She tried to imagine Glenmoor telling her such a thing, but could not. Surely the Duke had a stable in the country with many horses for riding and pulling carriages.

Perhaps the letter had been a lie. If so, she did not want to hear the truth. She liked the idea of a man who strolled through life at eye level rather than looking down on other people from his place in the saddle.

She had flipped back through a year's worth of letters, gorging herself on his writing for most of the afternoon, feeling her heart flutter as it had each time she'd seen his elegant script, especially when he had written her name. On the rare times he had called her Selina, rather than Mrs Ogilvie, she had been so overcome by the implications she had not slept for days.

Now she had married a man who should know her, but who seemed like a stranger. He called her Selina whenever he chose to. Perhaps there had been no special meaning to it at all.

Molly helped her into her nightgown, which they both knew had been found on the floor of the Duke's bedroom by his valet this morning. Selina could not decide how to feel about the fact. It was certainly not scandalous to visit the bed of one's husband. But then, everything they did now seemed to be of interest to the world.

She closed her eyes and sighed, then opened them again and looked at the door on the other side of the room. It was impossible to deny what she had done and how it had felt to be with him, which had been full of the wordless passion she had expected from the man who wrote her with such dedication. She was sure he would not object if she came to him again. Surely he would have said something if he had not liked what she had done.

She hesitated a moment more, then got out of the bed, stripping her nightgown over her head and dropping it at the foot of her own bed before opening the door and going into his room.

He was there as he had been on the previous day, naked beneath the sheets. But this time, the book had already been set aside and he was staring at her in the doorway, as if he had been listening for her steps. As their eyes met, he shifted, making room for her to climb in beside him. Then he threw back the sheet, revealing that he was already hard, as if the prospect of her arrival had been more than enough to excite him.

She climbed into bed and straddled him, but her position lasted for only a moment before he took hold of her ankle and rolled, trapping her on her back, under him.

For a moment, she was too shocked to do anything, not even breathe. He raised himself up on his elbows to look into her eyes and smiled in a knowing way that sent a tingle of expectation through her body. Then his lips came down upon hers in an unexpected kiss.

It was as heady and dangerous as the kiss in the sitting room had been. She felt her control disappear, her resistance to him evaporate as his lips touched hers and her mouth opened to let him take her fully, his tongue moving against hers in invitation.

This could not be happening. Last night, she had meant to keep herself apart from him, but after a day spent with Abbott and a night of love songs, her resistance was low and her surrender complete. She closed her eyes and focused her mind on the sensations rushing through her and not the man who was causing them, this stranger that she did not understand.

This was easier. She allowed her mind to float and the pleasure crest in waves as his hands found her breasts and took liberties that she had not allowed last night.

Why had she denied herself this? It had been so long since she had felt any touch other than her own. This was different. Unfamiliar, exciting and uniquely male. Possessive yet gentle. It was everything she'd imagined, when searching for hidden meanings in the mundane letters they'd shared. A man who knew her, body and spirit, had longed for her, held himself in readiness for the moment when they could finally be together.

The kiss continued, and she returned it, thrusting her tongue into his mouth and biting his lip and eliciting a low chuckle of satisfaction at her response. She had not touched him last night, other than to arouse him. But now she ran her hands over him, searching each muscle and sinew of his chest and arms, amazed at how hard he was and how soft it made her feel to be near him. Her legs relaxed, spreading for him, eager to accept all he had to give.

His hands smoothed down her sides before locking on to her hips, holding them steady as he rocked his erection against her, once, twice, three times, to remind her that she was not the only one ready for pleasure.

She remembered the feel of him filling her and could not help the eager sigh that escaped her lips as she kissed his throat, biting gently at the cords of his neck, rubbing her face against it, savouring the scent of him, soap and spice, exotic and intoxicating.

And then he was moving against her, sliding down her body, leaving a trail of kisses as he went, like a shower of rose petals, velvet soft against her body.

She felt a moment of surprise that was close to panic. In the past, with her husband, the act had been quick and a little one-sided. She had never experienced the feel of a man's lips making free with her.

She did not know, but that did not mean she had not imagined. In the past, she would take his letters to bed with her and pretend that they said so much more than they did. That he was there with her, as she stroked the paper lightly against her skin. She knew full well how to bring herself to life with her hands and she had imagined that, if they ever met, he would, too, teasing her with his fingers before he claimed her.

But kisses. So many kisses. Her breasts, her belly

and, oh, Lord, between her legs. She had heard whispers of such things, when married women had gathered to giggle over their lives. But she had not believed that it would happen to her, had been afraid to even suggest such a thing as seemed to be about to happen.

No. It was happening. He had spread her legs wide and was nuzzling her thighs, coming closer and closer to her most sensitive place before settling there with a nimble tongue and firm lips and soft breath. She was going to die, she was sure of it now, for no one could withstand a pleasure this intense and simply get out of bed and walk away from it. It was amazing.

It was everything she could have hoped it would be, from the letters he had sent her, kind and funny, always stopping just short of a promise that there might be more between them than just words.

But she had wanted more. And now, here it was, more than anyone had ever offered her. He was worshipping her, feasting on her, loving her as only he could.

And she was lost in it, spiralling tight as a watch spring, gasping and moaning, and finally crying out his name as the tension released.

'Abbott!'

He pulled away with a curse, leaving her cold and trembling as he demanded, 'Open your eyes.'

She had not realised they were closed. She opened them and looked up, thighs still quivering, and for a moment, she was baffled at the sight of Glenmoor, leaning over her, eyes dark with passion and rage.

Then she remembered the truth and turned her face away from him.

He put his fingers on her chin, turning her face back to his, staring into her eyes and daring her to look away again.

'My name is Alex,' he said. Then he laid a hand on her thigh, making the muscles jump with the remaining tension of her orgasm.

He slid into her then, hard and long, and it was as shockingly good as she had hoped it would be, as good as last night, even better than her imagination.

'Say my name.' His body was moving slowly against hers, but his voice was as tightly controlled as his movements.

She was silent, both excited and terrified, confused by the feelings that were raging in her. She wanted him, and yet she didn't. She wanted this. But she shouldn't.

'Say my name,' he said, in a tone that was rough with arousal.

'Alex,' she whispered, trying to look away.

'Again.'

Her muscles were tightening again, against logic and will. The slow hot friction was bringing her back to where she had been when his mouth had been on her, driving her wild. She stared at his lips, strange and yet intimately familiar, and felt the first shudder of passion wash over her.

'Again.' More urgent this time, his breath ragged with his own exertions.

'Alex,' she said, forcing the word out and gasping

as he came into her again. 'Alex.' But who was that, really? She did not know. But they were rushing towards something now that was impossible to stop and she would have said anything he asked if only to have that feeling again. 'Alex.'

He came into her, losing himself in one final thrust, taking her over the edge with him.

There was a moment of peace, then he rolled off her, on to his back, staring up at the ceiling.

She was afraid to look at him, yet she could not look away. He was beautiful, even if she did not want to admit it. He raised his hand, covering his eyes, and spoke without turning his head. 'You may go back to your room now.'

It was not a request. It was a demand, though spoken so softly that the pain it caused surprised her. After all that had happened, she did not think this man had the power to hurt her any more than he already had. She sat up and swung her legs out of the bed, and walked unsteadily to the door and through it, back to her own lonely bed.

She was not making love to him.

Alex wiped his face with his hand, as if he could wipe away the last few minutes, or perhaps the whole of the last year. Maybe, if he could begin again, it would be different. Or perhaps it would be better if he had never met her at all. But he was sure that he wanted to free himself of this thing he had created, this double who was so much more attractive to her than he could ever be.

It was against all logic, really. He was a duke, and a rich one at that. Educated as well. And, he had been told, more than moderately good-looking. To any other woman in the world, it would have been enough. But the one woman he wanted had to pretend he was someone else so that she could lie with him.

It was not fair. What they had just shared had been wonderful. At least, he'd thought they'd been sharing it. Instead, she had been thinking of someone else.

The fact that that someone else was just another part of him was the cruellest irony of all. He had created his own competition, a man who lived large in his wife's fantasy and was not beholden to the paltry rules of reality that chained Alex. Abbott had never hurt her. He did not gamble. He never made demands, nor did he drag her reputation through the mud. He gave and gave and never asked for anything in return. The man was perfect. There was no way to compete against that.

Why even try? From now on, the bedroom door would stay closed and locked, until she had a reason to seek *him* out and not some fantasy lover that he stood in proxy to. If they could not come together properly as man and wife, they would not be together at all.

Chapter Twenty

After a sleepless night, Selina came down to the breakfast room to find her husband in his usual spot, going through the morning post as if nothing had happened the night before. He was not smiling the secret smile he had worn yesterday morning, the one she had not appreciated when she'd had the chance.

Now she discovered she missed it and was not sure how to get it back. Did he expect her to apologise for what she had done last night? It had been an accident, but that was really no excuse for it. And it would not happen again. After how he had marked her with his lovemaking, she might never be able to close her eyes again, much less utter another man's name.

But had she really? It was a name he had chosen. It was him.

And yet, it was not.

Her hand trembled as she reached for the chocolate pot, for it was all very confusing and she was not ready to deal with it the first thing in the morning after worrying about it most of the night. But someone had to say something. The silence, which she thought she had grown used to, suddenly seemed too oppressive to bear.

'Do you have a horse?'

She sucked in a breath of surprise, for that had not been what she'd intended to say.

'I beg your pardon?' It had not been what he'd expected to hear either.

She cleared her throat. 'I said, do you have a horse?'

'No,' he said, looking at her as if she had just lost her mind.

'But you have carriage horses. And I assume there is a stable at your country home,' she pressed, unable to stop herself.

'There were horses there when I came into the title. Hunters, riders, carriage horses, dray horses.' He shrugged. 'I am unsure how many. More than are needed, I suspect. But there are none that I would call mine. I do not know their names or feed them sugar lumps and dote on them, as if they are large, stupid children. I have horses, but none that I hold any attachment to.'

'Oh.' That explained the letter, which was, in some sense, an accurate way to describe his preferences.

'Do you have any other questions?'

She had many. But the last was delivered in a way that said he had no desire to answer her frivolous queries, so she shook her head and went back to her chocolate.

He was silent, too, for a time. He helped himself to another cup of coffee, buttered a muffin and opened another letter, then spoke without looking up. 'Do you need any instruction in preparing for the card party? Have you chosen a date?'

She had not precisely forgotten yesterday's request. She had simply hoped that it might go away, especially after what had happened in bed. She wet her lips. 'I have done nothing, thus far.'

'It need not be large. Ten couples, more or less.'

It might as well have been a hundred for the dread she felt at the suggestion. 'It is not the size that upsets me,' she said, then challenged him. 'How large was the party where you met my husband?'

He looked up at her with an expression that said he'd said more than enough on this subject, then replied, 'It was not a party, nor was it at one of the seedy gaming hells you seem to think I inhabit. It was at White's. I have no idea how he gained entry there, as he was not a member. He must have been someone's guest. No one stepped forward to claim him, after what occurred. I am sure the person who led him to that final game was more than happy to see me get all the credit for it.'

'Oh,' she said softly. This was not what she had imagined at all.

'And he is not your husband,' the Duke reminded her. 'He is your first husband. Or perhaps your late husband.'

'I did not mean…' she began to say, then trailed off, embarrassed.

'Of course you didn't,' he said bitterly. Then he looked back at his plate, refusing to meet her gaze.

'Because of the location, I had no reason to distrust his marker, nor were the stakes so high that I meant to ruin him. It was a friendly game and in no way memorable.'

But he obviously remembered each detail of it. Perhaps she was not the only one haunted by what had occurred that night.

'I should have asked you before this,' she said softly.

'Yes, you should have,' he agreed without looking up. 'But from the moment we met, you have argued and misconstrued, and rebuffed me at every turn. You have spared no opportunity to remind me that I am not the man you wanted to marry.'

Why was she surprised at the pain in his voice? Hadn't her intent been to make him suffer in this marriage? But suddenly her plans seemed foolish and they were hurting her as much as they ever did him.

He pushed his plate aside and stood up, staring down at her. 'The fact that you do not want me no longer matters, nor will I torment you with my demands after this one. The card party will be my farewell to London society for the Season. After that, you and this city are welcome to each other.' Then he left the dining room, and she heard the front door slam behind him.

She sat in silence for a moment, unsure of what to do next. Last night, they had been as close as two human beings could be. Now he did not even want to be in the same city with her. The woman who she had been on the day of their marriage would have rejoiced at this news. Now she did not know what to make of it.

She finished her breakfast and went to the morning room, sitting down with her book of names and addresses, and prepared the guest list that he had asked for, paged through her calendar and found a date a week hence, then began writing invitations.

The mechanical process of putting words to paper was comforting, as long as she did not think of what she was writing. But that uncoupling was impossible when she reached the final sheet that was to go to Baxter. She had to force her hand to form the words of courtesy needed to invite him and she sealed the paper quickly and put it in the stack of finished letters, hoping that the toxic nature of the receiver would be dissipated by the company of the other invitations.

Once finished, she went back to her room, closed the door behind her and went to the writing desk to the stack of Abbott letters, paging through them, searching for something that would help her understand what was happening to her now.

But instead of the comforting passages that she usually found, she saw continual hints and reminders that, no matter how strong their friendship and her love for him, they could never be together. Abbott had told her over and over that it would not work. Apparently, he had been right.

She folded the letters, stacked them and retied the ribbon. Then she noticed the conspicuous absence of the letter she had written yesterday. She paged through the papers again, more frantically this time, then turned to her maid, who was straightening the gowns in the wardrobe. 'Where is the letter that was on the desk?' she said urgently.

'I put it in the post,' Molly said, blinking innocently back at her.

'You foolish girl...' But that was unfair. She was the foolish one for writing that letter at all to a man she knew did not exist. She shook her head in apology and said more calmly, 'I was not finished with it.'

'It was sealed,' the girl reminded her.

'That was my mistake,' Selina replied. 'Is it too late to get it back?'

Molly hurried down to the front hall and back again, shaking her head. 'It is long gone, Your Grace.'

Selina took a breath to calm herself. What was the worst that could happen? It would probably sit unclaimed at the post office that she had addressed it to, for what reason would Alex have to retrieve it? In case it did come here, she would watch the incoming post and snatch it back before her husband found it and opened it. The last thing she needed was this further proof that she was still dreaming of a man who would never come.

At his club, Alex sat with his paper, pretending to read and hoping that it would be enough to dissuade any of the other members from conversation. He should have gone to Gentleman Jackson's for some sparring instead. He felt like hitting something.

Or perhaps he felt like being hit. A few sharp jabs to his head might clear the fog and make it easier to see a way forward that didn't involve running from his wife like a coward. But was it really cowardice not to stay in a place he was not welcome or wanted?

And what was he going to do about Edward? The boy's mother might not want him, but the boy had grown to depend on him in a few short days. He would have to sit down with the child and tell him that Alex's departure had nothing to do with him. Perhaps he could teach the boy how to play chess by mail and they could still have their games.

Evan dropped into the chair next to him, pushing the paper away and staring at the wine glass on the table next to Alex. 'You are here early.'

'No earlier than you,' he replied, giving the paper a warning rattle.

'Responding to the invitation that was just hand delivered to my house. We will be there, of course.'

Apparently, his wife had taken him at his word and organised the event as he'd requested. 'The card party? And when are we holding it?'

Evan laughed. 'Shouldn't you be the one to tell me?'

'The calendar is Selina's purview, not mine.'

'Tuesday afternoon,' Evan replied, giving him an incredulous look.

'Five days' time, then,' he said thoughtfully.

'And was this Selina's idea as well? Because I would find that hard to believe,' Evan said, still staring at him.

'She arranged the party at my instruction.'

'And that is why you are out of the house now,' Evan said with a nod. 'Go home and say you are sorry.'

'I have nothing to be sorry for,' Alex snapped.

'Of course not,' his brother replied with a laugh. 'You are merely forcing your wife to play cards after she watched them destroy her life. Why would she be angry with you over that?'

'There is little I do that does not make her angry,' he said, annoyed at the note of self-pity in his voice. 'And it is all the fault of Abbott.'

Evan shook his head. 'I blame Oxford for giving you misguided views of male and female relations. Even I did not make such a hash of the early days of my marriage and I was decidedly wrong-headed.'

'Thank you for your assessment,' Alex said, glaring and reaching for his wine glass. 'I could never have come to that conclusion on my own.'

'And now, what do you mean to do about it?'

'Travel,' he said. 'Now that the war is over, I thought, perhaps a trip to Paris...'

'You are running away,' Evan said.

'I am merely putting sufficient space between myself and the woman I married.' But would the Channel be enough to ease the hurt. 'I am considering the Americas as well.'

'Or you could stay and make up for what you have done,' Evan suggested in a gentle tone.

'She ignores my actions and will not listen to a word I say.'

'Then you must do the obvious,' Evan said.

'And what is that?'

'Why don't you write her a letter?'

Chapter Twenty-One

The few days before the card party passed quickly, and there was little to do to prepare other than to plan a menu of light refreshments and locate enough tables and chairs for the players. There were no regrets in the responses to her invitations, as far as she knew.

When the answer from Baxter arrived, she could not bring herself to open it. Instead, she tossed it into her husband's pile of mail on the breakfast table and told him in a curt voice that he must deal with any correspondence with that man as she simply could not.

The Duke looked up at her without speaking, then popped the seal and scanned the response. 'He is coming,' he said, then went back to eating his breakfast.

They spoke little to each other, these days. Two weeks ago, she would have preferred the silence, but now it bothered her. There were things she needed to say to him and she was still not sure what they were.

Things were different in the evenings when they were home, for Edward was there and they had declared an unspoken truce while in his presence. She stayed on one side of the room and busied herself with her needlework and the Duke stayed on the other, where he continued to teach her son chess, training him on the notation of the spaces so he might understand how best to describe the moves he was making. It was all very civil and she suspected that Edward was not the least bit fooled by it.

Afterwards, they went to their respective bedrooms and closed their doors without saying goodnight. Then Selina lay awake, staring at the connecting door, afraid to touch it, lest she find it locked. Even if it was open, she did not think she had the nerve to go through it, though her body yearned to be with him again.

If he was going away, as he had threatened, would it be so wrong to be with him, one last time? Perhaps she could make him change his mind. But with the card party looming ever closer, it was impossible to think. Her head ached. Her stomach roiled. She could not sleep at night or focus during the day.

When the day of the party arrived, all she could manage was a sip of tea at breakfast before going to the sitting room to oversee the removal of the furniture and its replacement with game tables. Everything was properly in its place and the guests would be arriving in the early evening. All that was left was for her to dress and be ready to greet them.

And when she did, she would have to sit down with them, to shuffle and deal and pretend to be happy. She had seldom played and was not particularly skilled at any of the games the Duke was planning. She did not know how or when to bet at loo, and to be partnered with anyone for whist would be a disaster, since there was no way she could keep up with the subtleties of the play.

She slowly backed out of the room, then turned and hurried down the hall and up the stairs, unable to face the prospect any longer. Before going to her room, she stopped to see Edward in the nursery and he greeted her arrival with a sulky glare. 'You promised,' he said, folding his arms in front of his chest in a gesture of defiance.

'What, my darling?' she said, crouching down beside him.

'You said that the Duke had no problems and would not go away. But he has told me that he is going on a long trip and that I cannot come along.' The words tumbled out of him, his face going red with anger and unshed tears.

'But we will remain in his house,' she said patiently.

'Where is he going?' Edward said, stomping a foot. 'Is he going to the country house? He said I could go there. He said that we would all go there in summer.'

She had no idea how to answer, for the Duke had said nothing of his plans to her. 'I do not know,' she admitted, placing her hand on her son's shoulder. 'But I am sure he would take you along, if that was all he planned.'

'What did you do?' Edward demanded. 'What did you say to make him not like us any more?'

The accusation hurt, probably because it was so accurate a way to describe what had happened, and her silence proved to him that he was right.

'Can't you say you are sorry?' he said hopefully. 'Then perhaps he will not go.'

She had not. Perhaps it would not be enough, but perhaps it would. 'I will talk to him,' she said at last, not wanting to dash the boy's hopes.

He smiled back at her, offered her a hug, by way of a reward, and returned to the book he had been reading, confident that she would solve all their problems with a simple apology.

She walked out into the hall and to her room, her feet dragging at each step as she thought of the night that lay ahead. She had not wanted to do this when the Duke had first suggested it and she liked it no better now that the event was upon them.

She turned to the connecting door and listened to the faint sounds of movement on the other side. He was preparing for the party, just as she should be. She walked forward and put her hand on the door handle, rattling it in frustration when she discovered that it was locked. 'Alex,' she called. 'I need to talk to you.'

There was a moment of silence and then a mutter, as the Duke dismissed his valet. The door opened and he stood before her, staring expectantly.

'I am sorry,' she said. When he did not respond, she continued. 'Sorry for everything. For the way I have treated you, for not trusting you. And,' she whispered, 'for the thing I said in the bedroom.'

'But?' he replied. 'For there is clearly more you want to say to me.'

'I cannot do this,' she said, then added, 'I am ill.' And she did feel sick. It was not a lie.

'We have guests coming in an hour,' he reminded her in a calm voice.

'You have guests,' she countered. 'You know I cannot abide gambling. Please do not force me to do it. Anything but that.' And, for the first time since they had married, she could not stop the tears that were welling up in her eyes. She reached out for the doorframe as the world seemed to pitch and rock beneath her and her knees buckled.

'Damn.' He caught her before she could swoon, scooping her into his arms and carrying her back into her room to lay her on the bed. He laid a hand on her forehead, then rubbed her wrists as if trying to force life back into her. 'You have worked yourself into a state over this.' His voice was rough and annoyed, but not totally without sympathy. 'What have you eaten today?'

She answered with an embarrassed shrug, for it was long past luncheon and she'd had nothing at all.

He let out an exasperated sigh. 'I will give your regrets.' Then he walked to the bell-pull and summoned her maid with a sharp tug. 'Her Grace is ill. Feed her and put her to bed.'

Then he left her, embarrassed and alone.

Alex went back to his room and called for his valet to finish with his cravat and coat, trying to ignore the creeping guilt at the thought of the woman in the next room. He had dismissed her protestations over this event, but had never imagined that she would work herself into a state of nervous prostration over it.

He was not so great a villain as to force her to entertain when she might swoon at any moment, though it would certainly add that touch of melodrama that would earn them a place in tomorrow's paper. Instead, he would have to manage the event himself. Once he was dressed, he informed the servants of the change, checking on the menu and assuring himself that there was sufficient claret for the gentlemen and ratafia for the ladies.

Then he went to the entryway to greet his guests as they arrived. The footman at the door turned to him nervously and bowed, reaching into the pocket of his livery and offering a letter to Alex. 'From the lady, Yer Grace.'

He stared down at it, surprised to see that it was addressed to Mr Abbott. 'Where did you get this?'

'The post office, Yer Grace. You said I was to check the mail every day.'

And he had never told the fellow to stop, even after he had married Selina. Somehow, her last letter to him had fallen through the cracks and was only arriving now. 'Thank you for your dedication,' he said to the footman, stuffing the letter into the pocket of his own coat. 'It will no longer be necessary to go to the post office for me. There will be no more letters.'

The boy looked vaguely disappointed that he had lost such a special duty, but he nodded in obedience and went back to stand at the door as the guests began to arrive.

As usual, Evan and his wife were first. When they heard that Selina was indisposed, Maddie offered to stand in as hostess for the evening. They asked no questions, but he could see by the look they exchanged that they wanted to.

The other couples trickled in, including Selina's friend Mary Wilson and her husband. But he was waiting for the one person that Selina had wanted to avoid. When Alex had almost given up hope, Baxter appeared, pausing in the doorway to rake the foyer with his eyes.

'You are alone?' he said with a sly smile. 'I expected that the Duchess would be here to welcome me.'

'She is indisposed,' Alex said, gesturing towards the sitting room.

'How unfortunate. I so looked forward to seeing her.' The comment was no different from ones made by other guests. But somehow, when Baxter said it, it was vile.

Alex hid his feelings of disgust beneath a smile. 'Another time, perhaps. But now, if you will accompany me, the games are about to start.'

They went to the sitting room to find two chairs open at a table with Evan and Mr Wilson. It was exactly the setting that Alex had hoped for when he had planned the party and he took his seat and watched as Baxter picked up the deck.

'Fancy a game of loo?' Baxter was shuffling the

cards with an easy dexterity and smiling in what he probably thought was a welcoming way.

Alex smiled back, trying to conceal his loathing. 'Don't mind if I do.' He glanced at the other two men, who nodded in agreement and reached for their purses to throw coins into the pot.

Baxter dealt the cards. Then the play began.

Alex's hand was near to worthless and Baxter was a clear winner. He fared somewhat better in succeeding hands, only to lose again when Baxter dealt.

It was probably a coincidence. But it led him to watch more closely when the third round happened with the same results. There was something in the way Baxter held the cards that seemed wrong. Awkward, yet incredibly smooth. Without warning, he switched from riffling the cards to an overhand shuffle. Then dealt out Alex another worthless hand and took the pot again.

When it was Alex's turn to deal, he took a moment to feel the cards in his hands as he shuffled. Was there a faint bend in this card? A scratch on the back of that one? The deck had been new at the beginning of the evening, but now they seemed worn.

When it was Baxter's turn again, Alex waited until the man was about to begin dealing and called, 'Halt.'

Baxter froze, looking at him in confusion.

'Turn over the cards. I wish to see them.'

Baxter ignored him, ready to deal again.

'I said, I wish to see the cards,' he repeated, standing up and reaching across the table for them.

The other man instinctively pulled them back

towards his body, laughing nervously. 'Don't you trust me?'

'That remains to be seen,' Alex said, smiling back at him. 'Turn over the deck, please, so that we may see the source of your good luck.'

'This is ridiculous,' Baxter said, shaking his head. 'I have never...'

'Just show us the cards and be done with it,' Wilson said, staring at Baxter expectantly.

'Don't be ridiculous,' Baxter said, reaching to drop them into his pocket and end the game.

But Alex was too fast for him, grabbing his wrist and closing his other hand over the deck before Baxter could throw the cards away and hide the truth. Alex plucked the deck from his fingers, turning it over and fanning it out to reveal the aces placed neatly at the bottom.

He glanced from man to man, around the table. 'I suspect, if we examine the cards, we will find that they are bent or marked in some other way to make it possible for him to stack the deck.'

Curses rang out around the table and hands gripped Baxter, forcing him back into his seat as he tried to rise. 'Explain yourself,' said Evan. Around the room, play stopped and heads turned to watch the drama unfolding before them.

'Gentlemen,' Baxter said with a weak laugh. 'It is a strange coincidence. Nothing more than that.' Then he looked at Alex, as if daring him to make an accusation. 'Unless someone would want to imply that it is not.'

Alex laughed. 'Imply is such a gentle way to put it. I am stating quite plainly that you have been cheating at cards.' He pointed to Evan and Wilson. 'I know that these men are innocent and the deck that is now marked was fresh when we sat down to play. My only question now is, how long have you been playing us false and how many men have you cheated?'

Now the whole room was watching, fascinated.

'These are dangerous accusations,' Baxter said with a huff. 'As a man of honour...'

Alex held up his hand. 'Do you think to challenge a duke to an illegal duel? If you strike me down, you will hang for it. And personally, I would not waste a bullet on you, for you have no honour to offend. Now leave my house, or I will have you removed.'

'I have never been so insulted,' Baxter said, rising to go. But there was no strength to his words and he was unsteady on his feet as he made to go.

Before he could pass, Alex leaned in and said softly so that no one could hear, 'I told you if you harassed my wife again, I would ruin you. This is for that embarrassing on dit in the paper the morning after we gambled. I expect to hear no more from you. Now be gone.' Then, with a glance in their direction, he signalled the footmen by the sitting room door to see the fellow out.

The room stayed quiet for a moment, then everyone began talking at once, amazed by what they had just seen and eager to analyse each word.

After exchanging a satisfied look with Evan, Alex stood and spoke. 'I apologise for the rather colourful interruption in our fun. Let us refill our glasses and I will ring for the sandwiches. Then we shall have time for another hand.'

The play went on for another hour and a half and everyone declared that it had been a most enjoyable evening and very entertaining.

As the room cleared, Evan grabbed the last cheese sandwich off the tray on their table and said around a large bite, 'How long have you known that Baxter was a cheat?'

'I only suspected. I needed proof. If I had hinted at it before and been wrong? You know how quickly rumours spread.'

'The fellow is well and truly ruined now,' Evan said, satisfied. 'And all his previous wins are suspect.'

'If he is smart, he will pack his tricks and travel to the Continent. He will not be welcome in London for years to come.'

Evan laughed and Maddie tugged at his sleeve. 'We must leave now, for I expect Alex will want to tell his wife the good news. This discovery will lay to rest that nonsensical rumour that you took advantage of her late husband. Now everyone will see Mr Baxter as the villain.'

Alex could not help the smile, for that had been his hope all along. He had assumed that she would be in the room for the unmasking. But a second-hand tale would have to do. Then they would see if she wanted him to carry out his threat to leave her.

He saw his brother to the door, then went to his

study, to rehearse what he would say to her. The words, when he spoke them, must be better than anything he had managed when he had pretended to be Abbott.

It was then that he remembered the letter still in his pocket. Would it hurt to visit that part of his life one last time, when things had been less complicated and their love unconsummated and pure?

He cracked the seal and read.

My husband is not the man I thought he was. But neither is he you, and I do not believe he can be. How can I allow a man to touch my body who has never touched my heart? I fear that this marriage will be no different than the one I shared with John, an empty imitation of the union I seek.

He thrust the letter into the drawer where he saved the rest of the letters from her and slammed it shut. Then he went upstairs to pack, just as he had planned.

Chapter Twenty-Two

The next morning, Selina rose slowly, exhausted from the day before. It was true that she had not wanted to attend the card party on the previous evening and was glad that she had missed it. But neither had she intended to collapse weeping and be put to bed like an invalid. It was embarrassing and not at all like her.

But now that the party was over, they would be alone to deal with their own problems. She hoped that there was still time to convince the Duke to stay, as her apology had been weak and confusing, and not at all the cogent argument she had hoped to put forth for trying again.

Her maid came to her room to dress her and she paused for a moment before choosing a green day dress, remembering how much he'd remarked he liked her in green. If she was to live with him in any kind of harmony, she needed all the advantages she could find.

With her toilet completed, she went down to the breakfast room, only to find it empty. Was he avoiding her, or was he sleeping later than she had? She came back to the bedrooms, then, and knocked at the door of his room, only to have it opened by his valet.

'He was up with the dawn, Your Grace,' the man said with a subservient bow of his head. 'Then he went out and did not say where he was going.'

For a moment, she thought of John, who had sometimes stayed out for days and come home when his pockets were empty, smelling of strange perfume. Then she remembered that the Duke was a different sort of man. Even if he was not, it was hardly her place to object to how he wanted to spend his time. She smiled at the servant to prove that she found nothing unusual about her husband's behaviour, fighting down the nervousness it had raised in her. 'When he returns, tell him I wish to speak to him,' she said, then went to the nursery to see to Edward.

It was early afternoon and she was considering a nap when she received a visit from her friend Mary Wilson, who rushed into the room and enveloped her in a sisterly hug. 'Are you better today? What was wrong yesterday? We all missed you.'

'It was nothing,' Selina assured her. 'I was overtired. Nothing more than that.'

'I enjoyed it immensely, as did everyone I spoke to. And, of course, the latest on dit in the paper has cemented you as the most interesting couple of the Season.'

'Oh, dear,' Selina said, thinking of the argument that she'd had with the Duke and the possibility that one of the servants might have heard. 'What are they writing about now?'

Mary looked at her with wide eyes. 'Surely you have heard.'

'Heard what?' Selina said with a smile.

'Your husband did not tell you what occurred? He did not speak to you after everyone had left?'

'Really, I have no idea what you are talking about,' she said, becoming annoyed. What had the Duke done to raise such a fuss and why had he kept another secret?

'It was in the paper this morning and is in all the scandal sheets,' Mary supplied, shaking her head in amazement. 'Rumour has it that Baxter has fled the country to avoid the shame.' Then Mary's lips snapped shut and she covered her mouth. She was practically bouncing in her chair with excitement.

Selina sucked in a breath at the mention of the man's name before the full meaning of the sentence reached her. 'He has left England?'

Mary nodded. 'My husband was at the same table with the two Dukes and Baxter and assures me it was far more dramatic than the paper can convey. Your husband took the deck from his hand and proved that Baxter was dealing from the bottom. Baxter tried to bluff, even after he was caught, and threatened a duel. Your husband laughed at him and said that such things were for men of honour and that he was not worthy of a bullet. And then Baxter slunk off like the miserable cur he is. All of London wonders how long he has been cheating and whether he gained any of his winnings honestly.'

Her nemesis was vanquished, in an act so dramatic that the whole *ton* knew of it. It was the sort of romantic gesture that she had dreamed her hero Abbott would make for her. A public humiliation that had preserved her honour and avenged John Ogilvie.

'And I am sure we will hear no more nonsense about Glenmoor ruining your first husband,' Mary said with a solemn nod. 'Personally, I never believed it and I am sure you did not either. Not really, or you would not have married him.'

A lie of agreement was on the tip of her tongue and she bit it back, as the shame of the truth washed over her. 'That is just it, Mary. I blamed him. I always have. When I married him, I think it was more out of revenge than anything else. I wanted to hurt him and thought this might be the easiest way to do it.'

'But he was so kind to you,' her friend said, surprised. 'And didn't you say when he was writing you all those letters that you were friends? And I thought perhaps something more.'

'I did not know what to think, when I found out. I was so foolish. I read and read them, but I never imagined his hand holding the pen.' Or his face, smiling as he wrote, just as he had smiled at her on their wedding day, no matter how foul she was to him.

But she could see him now, though the image wavered in the tears that were filling her eyes. 'I was a fool,' she said, wringing her hands.

'You must tell him so,' Mary said softly, offering

her a handkerchief before she could ask. 'Is he in the house right now?'

'No. He has gone out, to Parliament, I think.' But that did not begin until afternoon. He had gone far too early for that.

'It is not in session today,' her friend corrected her.

'Oh,' she said faintly. 'He is probably at his club then. I am sure I will see him at supper and he will explain everything. Then I can tell him how wrong I have been.'

'Of course,' said Mary, giving her a sympathetic nod. 'And thank him for all of us, for handling Baxter with such skill. The man is hated throughout London.'

When her friend left, she hurried upstairs to find the Duke's valet to enquire as to whether he had returned without her noticing. That man knew nothing, but admitted that two suits of clothes were missing and enough linen to last for a week. Wherever he had gone, he did not intend to come back anytime soon.

'And he would not have gone to the country without me,' the valet insisted, his brow creased with worry.

'I am sure it is nothing we need to be concerned about,' Selina said, experimenting with a brave smile to show that it was just a tiff that they would settle in time.

But was that the case? She did not think so. She had wasted so much time blaming Alex for John's death, no matter how many times he had insisted that it was not his fault. Why had she not seen Baxter for the villain he was? If he had won the house by cheating, he owned the lion's share of the blame for what happened after.

And John was to blame as well. The Duke had been blunt in his assessment of her late husband and she had felt the need to defend him. But what John had done must be viewed through the lens of his own affliction. There had been nothing right or fair about his treatment of her. Blind obedience to a dead man served no purpose, especially when there was a living man in her life who had done nothing but try to help.

She thought of the way she had treated him and she got a sick feeling in the pit of her stomach that only grew worse as she imagined each interaction and how desperately she had clung to John, though he had done nothing to deserve her devotion.

She had punished the Duke of Glenmoor unfairly. Even after she had learned how much he had helped her. Lord knew why he was so kind to her through it all. And, without her asking, he had continued to uncover what had happened on the night John had died, to bring the facts of it before the *ton*. How could she ever thank him?

For now, she had to find him, to talk to him and try to make right some of the things she had done wrong. She thought of them in bed together and the fiery passion they shared. If she could put her girlish fantasies aside, and stop longing for the man in his letters, she could be a good wife to him, she was sure. But first, she must find him.

She ran down the stairs, then down the hall and

into his study, hoping that he had left some clue behind there. His desk was orderly and spotless, though there was a pile of books on the shelf that had not been put away, as if he kept them out to refer to them frequently.

She ran a hand over the spines and read the titles. Philosophy, poetry, Shakespeare. Food for an enquiring mind with perhaps a touch of romance in the soul. They were the sorts of things she had imagined Abbott would have had in his study, for he had claimed to be a romantic at heart. Their presence made her smile, for, though he did not seem to want to be associated with that name, the spirit of his letters resided somewhere within him.

She opened a desk drawer, looking for other clues. The first was uninteresting, holding ledgers and unpaid bills, and correspondence with his man of business. But in the second drawer, the one at his right hand so the contents were close at all times, was a stack of crisp fresh paper, devoid of monogram or crest, a bottle of blue ink and a pair of freshly sharpened quills.

Her heart quickened at the sight, for it was as if she were looking into another desk entirely. Abbott's desk. She could imagine him taking out the makings of a letter to her, pushing his work to the side to indulge himself in the joy of writing.

Then she rejected the fantasy. She was far too guilty already of attributing motives to the man without asking him his mind. Maybe he had viewed those letters as a chore. He certainly seemed to think that the persona was unwanted baggage, now that she knew the truth. Maybe he was ashamed of the time he had wasted on her.

But perhaps there was something here that would tell her the truth. The stack of paper was not as flat and symmetrical as it should be. When she riffled through it, she could see several folded sheets tucked between the unused ones, as if he had wanted them out of sight even in the already private space they occupied.

She was not supposed to see them. But neither should she be in this room, going through his desk. What was one more sin on top of the first? She pulled the papers out of the stack and smoothed them flat, reading.

My dearest Selina,

This had been crossed out, then replaced with the same words again, followed by the admission,

That is what you are to me, though I have been too cautious to write the words before. You are dearest to me and grow dearer with each passing day. Your name is like a poem, a refrain that rings over and over in my head each time I see you, and each time I sit down to write.

How I long to say the word aloud, rather than hiding behind the courtesy of your married name. Selina.

By now, you know the reason why I have not

come to you or made the offer I think you hoped for. If you know, you hate me, which confirms my need for secrecy.

Please believe that it was never my intention to trick you. Our correspondence began as something simple and I intended it to be brief. But I enjoyed your letters so much that I could not seem to stop. A dozen times at least I wrote a letter that I hoped would be the last, only to write another the next day.

And a dozen times I wrote a letter proclaiming my love for you, admitting all. And each time, I tossed them into the fire. I was too great a coward to confess and too self-indulgent to give you up.

Now you are mine. And yet, you are further away than ever.

What shall I do with you, Selina? You come to me pale as a shaft of moonlight and offer your body freely. But I fear your soul belongs to another. That man. A man I can no longer be for you.

Abbott was an illusion, a man without a past that he needed to atone for. But I, my darling, am all too human and I fear that will never be enough for you.
Your adoring husband,
Alexander Fitzgerald Conroy

He had written it recently, just as she'd written to him. She ran her finger along the lines of text, hearing his voice as she read. She stared at the script, the hand so familiar, like dozens of letters that she had received and cherished. She could set it beside the others and know that all the words had come from the same man. The only difference between this and the previous notes was the name at the bottom, the name of her husband, the man who would admit to a depth of feeling that Abbott had never claimed for her.

Why had she not remembered what he had said of the Duke while in his disguise? He had hinted that Glenmoor could not behave normally in her presence. That he was stunned by her beauty until he was unable to talk. And if she had to describe him, he was still a taciturn man, more comfortable with Edward than he was with her.

But what did he need to say? She knew him through a year of letters. If all he had said in them was true, then she knew him better than she had John. He was her soulmate, after all.

Another proof of that was the familiar bundle of familiar papers, tied neatly with a cord, that had been pushed to the back of the drawer. He had kept her letters to re-read, just as she had kept his.

And there, at the top, was the foolish note she had written to Abbott a week ago, when she had been sure that her marriage could never be happy. He had received it and read it, and now he was gone.

She had driven him away with her own words.

The bottom seemed to drop out of her world as it had yesterday, while she was poised in the doorway between their rooms and had been suddenly too weak to stand. She had needed him then to care for her and she needed him now. What would she do, now that he was out of her reach? How could she apologise? How could she make this better?

In the distance, the front door slammed and she heard footsteps pounding down the hall and her husband, Alex, her beloved, calling her name. He stopped in the doorway of the study and they stared at each other in equal confusion, embarrassed by the emotions that racked them.

'Your Grace,' she said in a shocked gasp.

'Selina?' The name was a question, as if he did not know what to do with her, now that he'd found her.

'You left without telling anyone where you were going,' she said, still breathless.

'I did not think it would matter,' he replied.

'You did not even tell your valet,' she reminded him. 'He is beside himself.'

'Harvey fears that I will travel without a clean shave and fresh linens. He always worries about me.' His lips quirked into a smile at the idea.

'And he is not the only one,' she said, pausing and wetting her lips.

'Really,' he said, eyeing her and waiting for any sign that she might say more. 'Edward, I suppose.'

'He is most fond of you and was overwrought to think that you might go away,' she said, blinking at him. 'I wanted to tell you that yesterday. But I failed.'

He took a step into the room. 'And was that all?' he asked, searching her face.

'And I heard what you did with Baxter. It will change the way society views you,' she said.

'If I cared about the *ton*, it would please me to know that,' he said, still staring at her.

'I care,' she said, and it came out in a whisper.

'I beg your pardon?' He cupped a hand to his ear.

'It matters to me that people think well of you. And that they understand that you did nothing wrong when you and John played cards. I know that now.'

He closed the door and took another step closer.

'I was wrong,' she said, her voice growing stronger. 'About so much. But my life changed so suddenly. And I did not want to blame John, because one should not speak ill of the dead. And to admit that there were problems between us was like admitting that my life had been wasted.' She hesitated, trying to find the rest of the words that would make him believe her. 'This would be better in a letter.'

'I think we have both had far too many of those,' he said with a sad look, and turned again.

'I read yours,' she said. 'The one in your desk.'

He flinched.

'And I know that you read mine. I was not myself when I wrote that. I never meant for you to see it.'

'You wrote it to me,' he reminded her, with a frustrated shake of his head.

'I was not ready to give up what we had together,' she said, struggling to explain. 'And I was confused. Because you were everything I had hoped for, Alex.'

At the sound of his name, something changed in

him. Though he did not move, he felt closer to her, more open to her words.

She went on. 'But I was afraid that you weren't telling the truth when you wrote to me. That you made it up, like you made up Abbott.'

'I have never lied to you,' he said softly.

'Then your last letter is true,' she said, smiling hopefully at him. 'You love me.'

'Always. Ever. Still.' He shook his head helplessly and took another step towards her.

'When I read it, I saw all of you,' she said, spreading her hands wide. 'Both Abbott and Alex. I saw you and I knew I loved you, too.'

He closed the last few steps between them, leaning over the desk to give her a kiss that was as possessive as anything she had imagined in the long months when she'd been falling in love with him. She surrendered to it, wrapping her arms around his neck, clinging to him, still half afraid that he would change his mind again and leave her.

When he pulled away, they were both panting and his eyes blazed into hers.

'I love you, Alex,' she said, smiling up at him. 'And when I was afraid I had lost you, I did not know what to do or how to find you. Do not ever do that again.'

'I was halfway to Portsmouth when I turned around,' he said, leaning down to kiss her again. 'I had some half-baked idea that I would board a ship for Boston.'

'I am glad you didn't,' she said, stroking his face and kissing his cheek, surprised at how familiar it felt, as though she'd known him all her life. 'But what made you decide to come back to me?'

'The item in the paper about us,' he said, smiling.

'About Baxter?' she said, confused.

He shook his head. 'The gossips seem to think that your absence last night was proof that you were in a delicate condition. And I thought, if it might be true, I could not leave you.'

She laughed, kissing him quickly on the lips. 'I suppose it is possible. But I would hope that I would know before the rest of the *ton*. And as yet…?' She shrugged. 'It is far too soon to assume.'

'But it is not impossible. We have, after all…' He was blushing and it made her laugh.

She stood up then and came around the desk to settle in his arms. 'You ought to know that you cannot believe everything you read in the papers.'

'True, I suppose,' he said. 'But since it is such happy news, I suggest we celebrate our good fortune.' He smiled and kissed her again in a way that left no doubt as to his intentions. Then he went to lock the door.

* * * * *

Get 3 FREE REWARDS!

We'll send you 2 FREE Books <u>plus</u> a FREE Mystery Gift.

FREE Value Over **$20**

Both the **Harlequin® Historical** and **Harlequin® Romance** series feature compelling novels filled with emotion and simmering romance.

YES! Please send me 2 FREE novels from the Harlequin Historical or Harlequin Romance series and my FREE Mystery Gift (gift is worth about $10 retail). After receiving them, if I don't wish to receive any more books, I can return the shipping statement marked "cancel." If I don't cancel, I will receive 6 brand-new Harlequin Historical books every month and be billed just $6.19 each in the U.S. or $6.74 each in Canada, a savings of at least 11% off the cover price, or 4 brand-new Harlequin Romance Larger-Print books every month and be billed just $6.09 each in the U.S. or $6.24 each in Canada, a savings of at least 13% off the cover price. It's quite a bargain! Shipping and handling is just 50¢ per book in the U.S. and $1.25 per book in Canada.* I understand that accepting the 2 free books and gift places me under no obligation to buy anything. I can always return a shipment and cancel at any time by calling the number below. The free books and gift are mine to keep no matter what I decide.

Choose one: ☐ **Harlequin Historical** (246/349 BPA GRNX) ☐ **Harlequin Romance Larger-Print** (119/319 BPA GRNX) ☐ **Or Try Both!** (246/349 & 119/319 BPA GRRD)

Name (please print)

Address   Apt. #

City   State/Province   Zip/Postal Code

Email: Please check this box ☐ if you would like to receive newsletters and promotional emails from Harlequin Enterprises ULC and its affiliates. You can unsubscribe anytime.

Mail to the Harlequin Reader Service:
IN U.S.A.: P.O. Box 1341, Buffalo, NY 14240-8531
IN CANADA: P.O. Box 603, Fort Erie, Ontario L2A 5X3

Want to try 2 free books from another series? Call 1-800-873-8635 or visit www.ReaderService.com.

*Terms and prices subject to change without notice. Prices do not include sales taxes, which will be charged (if applicable) based on your state or country of residence. Canadian residents will be charged applicable taxes. Offer not valid in Quebec. This offer is limited to one order per household. Books received may not be as shown. Not valid for current subscribers to the Harlequin Historical or Harlequin Romance series. All orders subject to approval. Credit or debit balances in a customer's account(s) may be offset by any other outstanding balance owed by or to the customer. Please allow 4 to 6 weeks for delivery. Offer available while quantities last.

Your Privacy—Your information is being collected by Harlequin Enterprises ULC, operating as Harlequin Reader Service. For a complete summary of the information we collect, how we use this information and to whom it is disclosed, please visit our privacy notice located at corporate.harlequin.com/privacy-notice. From time to time we may also exchange your personal information with reputable third parties. If you wish to opt out of this sharing of your personal information, please visit readerservice.com/consumerschoice or call 1-800-873-8635. **Notice to California Residents**—Under California law, you have specific rights to control and access your data. For more information on these rights and how to exercise them, visit corporate.harlequin.com/california-privacy.

HHHRLP23